T0158410

You as of Today
My Homeland

You as of Today My Homeland

STORIES OF WAR, SELF, AND LOVE

Tayseer al-Sboul

Translated by Nesreen Akhtarkhavari

MICHIGAN STATE UNIVERSITY PRESS | *EAST LANSING*

♾ The paper used in this publication meets the minimum requirements
of ANSI/NISO Z39.48-1992 (R 1997) (Permanence of Paper).

Michigan State University Press
East Lansing, Michigan 48823-5245

Printed and bound in the United States of America.

22 21 20 19 18 17 16   1 2 3 4 5 6 7 8 9 10

LIBRARY OF CONGRESS CATALOGING-IN-PUBLICATION DATA
Sabul, Taysir.
[Anta mundhu al-yawm. English]
You as of today my homeland : stories of war, self, and love / Tayseer al-Sboul ;
translated by Nesreen Akhtarkhavari.
pages cm.—(Arabic literature and language series)
Includes bibliographical references.
ISBN 978-1-61186-210-2 (cloth : alk. paper)—ISBN 978-1-60917-496-5 (pdf)—
ISBN 978-1-62895-269-8 (epub)—ISBN 978-1-62896-269-7 (kindle)
I. Akhtarkhavari, Nesreen, translator. II. Sabul, Taysir. Short stories. Selections.
English. III. Title.
PJ7862.A2834A5813 2016
892.7'36—dc23
2015033654

Book design by Charlie Sharp, Sharp Des!gns, Lansing, MI
Cover design by Shaun Allshouse, www.shaunallshouse.com
Cover image of the sand dunes of Wadi Rum Desert, also known as
The Valley of the Moon, in southern Jordon is used with permission
(dreamstime.com/Demerzel21/ ID 44503621).

Michigan State University Press is a member of the Green Press Initiative and is
committed to developing and encouraging ecologically responsible publishing
practices. For more information about the Green Press Initiative and the use
of recycled paper in book publishing, please visit *www.greenpressinitiative.org*.

Visit Michigan State University Press at *www.msupress.org*

My friend, I
walk in a dream, aware
wander toward the edge of death.
A strange prophet I am, who left
with no destination in mind.
I will fall. Darkness will no doubt fill my soul,
a dead prophet, who has yet to reveal a verse.
You are my friend,
I know, but my path has changed.
I ask your forgiveness, just in case
we ever meet in a dream.
But you will rise the next day and forget.
How often you forget!
Peace Be Upon You.

—Tayseer al-Sboul, written in 1973
shortly before his suicide

CONTENTS

PROLOGUE

Otba Al-Sboul

A stunning chain of events in May 1967 led to a new war in the Near East. In just six days (June 5–10), a newly born state, Israel, not only crushed three Arab armies (Egypt, Jordan, and Syria) but also conquered an area three-and-a-half times larger than Israel itself! The Six-Day War changed the region. As mentioned in a 2007 article in *The Economist*,[1] most Israelis, intoxicated by the "complete victory" and alleviated from the fear of a second Holocaust, saw a divine hand giving a green light to an irredentist religious-nationalist movement intent on permanent siege of the occupied lands.

The "complete defeat and humiliation" of the Arabs not only shattered Pan-Arab dreams but also gave rise to Islamic fundamentalist groups, who saw a divine hand punishing people and leaders alike for failing to follow their interpretation of Islam. Almost fifty years after the war, the region is still trying to comprehend, let alone to reconcile, the full consequences of those traumatic times.

My father, Tayseer, like many in his generation, was totally shocked and devastated by this war. As he was trying to make sense out of the events, he embarked on a personal existential journey and submitted his own testimony in the form of a novella, "You as of Today."

Nesreen Akhtarkhavari approached our family in 2012 with a proposal to translate the novella into English. As excited as we were by the idea, we voiced concerns that it was going to be quite challenging. The novella is full of historical, religious, and cultural references that make it almost untranslatable.

But in hindsight, I can confidently say that my family is extremely grateful to Dr. Akhtarkhavari for not being thwarted. Despite tremendous challenges, she managed to accurately translate my father's novella. Now with this edited version of the translation; the translation of two of his short stories, "The Rooster's Cry" and "Red Indian"; and her and Anthony Lee's translation of my father's poetry in *Desert Sorrows*, Tayseer's work can carry its messages to a wider audience.

As a persistent, talented academic translator committed to her work, Dr. Akhtarkhavari not only translated the work but also conducted extensive research to accurately understand and depict the period and the people involved, especially Tayseer himself. Furthermore, she formed a personal bond with Tayseer friends, our family, and even my father—as he saw himself—ignoring my recurrent playful advice to not get dragged into "Tayseer's world."

In November 1973, at thirty-four years of age, Tayseer decided to take his own life. It was an act that not only left our family and friends with unhealed scars but also deprived the region and the world of a unique literary perspective that could have had helped us in exploring some answers and possible solutions to troubling questions. Is there a future to the Near East Region? Or are we just doomed to live in a nightmarish Eagles' "Hotel California," where "we are all just prisoners here of our own device" and where "you can check out anytime you like, but you can never leave"?

NOTE

1. "Israel's Wasted Victory: Six Days of War Followed by 40 Years of Misery. How can it ever end?" *The Economist*, May 24, 2007.

INTRODUCTION

Tayseer al-Sboul (1939–1973) was one of the Arab world's most talented writers and reformers. His work is widely recognized in the region and has had a significant impact in modernizing the Arabic novel. He is a popular figure studied and referenced by writers and academics alike, especially in Jordan.[1] In celebration of his contribution to literature, the Jordanian Writers Society created an annual award in his honor, and universities hold literary conferences in his name.[2] His poems are quoted in songs.[3] His novella, "You as of Today," brought recognition to Jordanian writers when it won the prestigious Al-Nahar Award for the Best Arabic Novel in 1968. This work became a model of reform in the Arabic novel and was widely celebrated in the region for its quality, content, and innovative style.

Al-Sboul's work, especially his novella, has been repeatedly recommended for translation by Arab writers and scholars.[4] Yet, it was not until 2001 that al-Sboul was first introduced to an English-speaking audience through a critical essay by Ahmad Majdoubeh in the *Journal of Arabic Literature*.[5] Majdoubeh described the novella as a pioneering and creative postmodernist project that altered the course of Arabic novels. The article provided a brief analysis of the work and listed references that illustrated the recognition it had achieved among Arab writers, critics, and academics.

In 2012, following a request from the Jordanian Writers Society, I translated the novella into English.[6] With the support of the Jordanian Ministry of Culture, it also was translated into French.[7] These translations remained local, with little circulation in the West. Then, in 2015, poet Anthony Lee and I translated al-Sboul's poetry collection, *Desert Sorrows*, into English.[8]

Al-Sboul's work is now accessible to English readers and provides a unique Arabic Jordanian experience that crosses the boundaries of time, place, and culture to celebrate our shared humanity.

Al-Sboul's work is rich in authentic content and frank in its treatment of critical social and historical issues that many shy from approaching. It presents the struggles, hopes, and shattered dreams of a generation of Arab youth, many of which are still relevant today. His innovative form, sophisticated and beautiful language, and skill as a writer make his work exceptional. The honesty and intensity by which he treats his subjects render it hard to separate fiction from reality. Like other great writers that he admired, al-Sboul was consumed with his people's struggles.[9] He wrote about their sufferings and unveiled the perceptions that governed their actions and reactions. His wife, May al-Yateem, described him as "a man destined to be a creative poet, transparent and sensitive, honest with himself and others, ideal, romantic, and keenly aware of his surroundings." She further explained, "His very short, brilliant life was a bitter record of the events and tragedies that took place in the larger Arab world."[10] Al-Sboul's close friend, Sadiq abd al-Haq, asserts that al-Sboul's work reflects events and circumstances that he actually experienced.[11]

ABOUT HIS LIFE

Al-Sboul was born on January 15, 1939, in Tafilah, a relatively remote town on the edge of the southern Jordanian desert. His father was a strong, traditional man with a firm connection to his land and culture. His mother was the youngest of three wives, a kind, soft-spoken woman from Khalil, a city on the West Bank of the Jordan River. The youngest of nine siblings, Tayseer was a sensitive boy, a distinguished student, and a poet.

In spite of his limited formal education, Tayseer's father was keen to educate his children. Tayseer left home to join his brother, Shawkat, an engineer and high-ranking officer in the Jordanian Army, to attend school. His new home in the military camp near the industrial city of Zarqa was a deep contrast to the wide open space of his village. After middle school, he attended high school in the capital city of Amman. During this period, he was significantly influenced by the city's active political scene and Shawkat's activism. Tayseer was greatly affected when Shawkat was arrested and imprisoned for his participation in the political struggle for Jordan's independence from Britain.[12] These early experiences are present throughout Tayseer's work.[13]

Upon graduating from high school, Tayseer was awarded a scholarship from the government to study philosophy at the American University of Beirut. With its modern, Westernized lifestyle, Beirut frustrated him, but it also helped him better define who he was and what he wanted. This period, inspired a number of his works, including "Red Indian," which expressed his rejection of Beirut's culture and departure from a naive infatuation with the white West, especially the United States.[14]

From Beirut, al-Sboul moved to Syria, which suited him better with its traditional society, Arab nationalist sentiments, and active political scene. There, he studied law at the University of Damascus, became politically involved, and published his creative work extensively in Syrian and Lebanese newspapers, as well as prominent Arab literary magazines, such as *al-Thagafah*, *al-Adab*, and *al-Adib*. The collection of his poems, *Desert Sorrows*, was also published in Beirut.[15]

After completing his studies in Damascus, al-Sboul married May al-Yateem, a writer and physician with Syrian and Bahraini roots, and returned to Jordan. There he worked in various government jobs, as well as took short-term positions in Bahrain and Saudi Arabia. After that, he returned to Jordan and opened a private law practice in the city of Zarqa. He soon closed the practice and accepted a position as a writer, producer, and host of a radio talk show called *With the New Generation*. His show gained popularity for featuring up-and-coming Arab and Jordanian writers and poets and for carrying on meaningful and relevant conversations. He worked at the radio station until his passing in 1973.

ABOUT THIS WORK

This book includes the translation of the most famous of al-Sboul's works, his novella "You as of Today"—one of the first historical fictions written in reaction to the 1967 War—as well as his two short stories, "Red Indian" and "The Rooster's Cry." The title of the novella is based on the lyrics of a patriotic song, "You as of Today Are Mine My Homeland," that Tayseer sang emphatically on his way from visiting the site of the broken bridge over the river that separated the East and West Banks of Jordan. Despite the destruction that he witnessed, he was still hopeful. He was thinking of moving forward and continuing the search for a way to make his nation great again. Inspired by this connection and the content of the novella and the two stories, we chose the title of this translation: *You as of Today My Homeland: Stories of War, Self, and Love.*

"You as of Today," is the main feature of this translation. As the prominent and prolific Jordanian writer Ghalib Halasa explains, the novella is unique because it realistically captures peoples' moods while world-changing events were taking place and reflects the true nature of everyday life.[16] Al-Sboul narrated history as he saw it happen. The protagonist explains that he was not "forcing history into the narrative," that the stories have actually happened. This connection between reality and fiction is evident throughout al-Sboul's work.[17] Wars and the charged political and social climate—started by the 1948 War and the events that followed, leading up to the 1973 accord—with conflicting ideologies and shifting loyalties strongly affected al-Sboul, as it did many in his generation. According to his wife, "on a personal level, Tayseer al-Sboul's great and shining life was void of any especially significant events.

His life moved through the same patterns that the youth of his generation went through. The major events that took place in the Arab world are what shaped Tayseer's life and directed it."[18] These conflicts rocked his world with a series of vicissitudes that began with false promises of victory and ended in defeat and disappointment. "He cried bitterly after the defeat [of the 1967 War] and went to the shattered bridge [that connected Jordan's East and West Banks] to say goodbye to a part of his homeland, very dear to his heart, which was lost forever."[19] When the world around him verged on the absurd, he "stopped writing poetry and started carefully reading history, looking for possible solutions or interpretations that might help him face what he saw as a dark and gloomy future."[20] During this period, he wrote "You as of Today" in an attempt to come to terms with the realities taking place in his private and public life. His journey back into history enriched his writing, providing an added depth and dimension. He skillfully wove symbols and events rooted in Arab religious and literary traditions, historical references, and cultural heritage into the narrative. Al-Sboul was eager to connect the past to the present in a continuum that he hoped would establish positive trajectories for a brighter future.

In addition to the novella's rich war content, al-Sboul tackled the forces that shaped the public sphere. He shared with the readers the intimate dreams and fears of a young Jordanian Arab with a nagging urge to find his great nation. With brutal honesty, vulnerability, and daring boldness, he exposes events and emotions, shocking at the time but genuinely humane. His descriptions of daily life bravely and artfully took on major issues such as migration, religion, tradition, family ties, gender relations, sex, prostitution, and domestic violence. In a bold move, and in spite of his full awareness of strong social taboos, censorship, and the volatile political atmosphere, he addressed political corruption, lack of freedom, violence, oppression, and the absence of due process, without concern for the price that he might have to pay.

Al-Sboul was as bold in his writing style as he was in the issues he addressed.

His novella did not adhere to the structure of traditional novels but followed a postmodernist approach. This makes it seem fragmented to some readers, but this fragmentation in structure, as Muhammad Obaid Allah explains, was "conscious and intentional" and "is not a reflection of the writer's lack of skills or ignorance of the rules of constructing a classical narrative."[21] As Ghalib Halasa writes, al-Sboul's novella "reflects in its structure the fragmentation in an integrated novel: short successive images, not linked by time, place, or a single event . . . connected through recalls that subject the images and the feelings of the moment to this recall process."[22] This structure allowed the author to freely dismantle, analyze, and reconstruct the world around him from within—as he experienced it.

The creative form of the novella, with its complex rhetoric, intertwined structure, and varied topics, became a model for a new style of Arabic narrative.[23] The threads of the chapters are carefully woven together with small repeated hints that connect the narrative and produce a coherent whole. The story is told by two narrators, with no clear distinction between them. The first narrator is the protagonist named Arabi Ibn Arabi, which literally translates to "an Arab and a son of an Arab." The second narrator is also an Arab, whose voice is allowed to arbitrarily interject, explain, and add to the narrative. The protagonist and the second narrator have a common understanding and a common destiny as closely tied as the destiny and worries of an Arab and his nation.

In the beginning of the novella, al-Sboul describes the protagonist's world. Through culturally rich scenes, the characters of the father, the mother, the comrade, and the hero brother turned petty thief and the world they operate in evolve. Arabi gradually reveals the rest of the world he lives in, with its complexity, including his personal struggle and sexual frustration as a male Arab youth in a culture with conflicting treatment of freedom and control, torn between tradition and Western ideologies. Slowly, the protagonist's commitment to his nation and his awareness of the nature of politics and social realities take shape. The private and the public intertwine, and events expose the triviality and lack of true leadership among the political elite and highlight the impact of it all on the young protagonist's idealistic dream of establishing a great nation that he would be proud to call his own.

The novella projects the intense escalation of the protagonist's personal and political turmoil from failed relationships with the opposite sex—including the housekeeper, the neighbor, and the prostitute—to his dysfunctional family and corrupt political leadership. The narrative depicts the struggle for power and position among opposing forces that leave Arabi and the other characters confused and lost. With that, the protagonist—like many in his generation and the generations of Arab youth today—is aware of the intensity of the social and political problems that plague his society and attempts to understand them, only to discover that they are too complicated and absurd. As a result, everything in his world crumbles and spins out of control. His feeling of crisis deepens. He returns to his old neighborhood looking for safety in the familiar. Desperate, he observes the escalating conflict between religion and politics as they occupy the public sphere and watch them destroy his world. He endures censorship and political oppression and watches his brother's greed destroy their small family, adding to his despair, alienation, and inner turmoil.

The two final chapters describe the 1967 War and the impact of the defeat—a nation drowned in confusion and sorrow, citizens frightened and desperate. The protagonist and the narrator analyze and explain events, sharing perspectives, feelings, and inner thoughts. This renders al-Sboul's novella not only a literary work but also a record of a nation that found itself engulfed in a moment out of the "Dark Ages."

Despite the overall success and popularity of the novella, al-Sboul remained humble. He never boasted about its success and was even shy when sharing it with others. He considered the process of writing it to have been a serious journey that changed his life. Explaining through the protagonist his motive to write, he said, "I write it because it bothers me."

The two short stories in the book, "Red Indian" and "The Rooster's Cry," did not receive the same attention as the novella. Nevertheless, they complement it, reinforce themes presented in al-Sboul's other works (his poetry, plays, and essays), and provide additional insights into the inner landscape of struggle and conflict facing the Arab man in his search for self and identity.

"Red Indian," the second and shortest work in this book, tells the story of a Jordanian youth's journey toward self-discovery and independence, away from the influence of his stubborn, patriarch father. The story mainly takes place in the Westernized part of Beirut in the mid-sixties and early seventies, the time al-Sboul lived and studied in the city. It is loaded with rich linguistic, social, cultural, and gender related issues that highlight the conflict and social distance between Eastern and Western cultures. Al-Sboul's bold language, which might seem offensive at times; his willingness to self-criticize; and his absolute honesty are clearly present in this short story. Despite its light content, the story analyzes and critiques important social and political issues, including the false perception of belonging to a Western culture that in reality sees Arabs as native savages. The conclusion of the story reaffirms al-Sboul's pride in being a Jordanian Arab and his contention with Western cultures' glaring whiteness and the superior attitude of its people.

The final work in this book, "The Rooster's Cry," focuses on a prisoner's encounter with the world outside prison on the evening of his release and the day after, and his attempt to function within his new realities. The story is an intimate journey that probes into the soul of the Arab man and his vulnerability, engulfing it all in a cloak of intense humanity. His struggle to find a moment of comfort is achieved only through his connection with the female protagonist, his friend's wife. He needs her to soothe his fragile body and mend his broken spirit. He justifies his transgression as rejection of what the friend has come to represent—an overweight, boring, greedy, and opportunist capitalist and a social pariah. Like in much of other Arab socialist writers' works, the woman becomes the savior of a broken and tormented man.[24]

In the novella and the two short stories, al-Sboul departs from the self-glorification commonly practiced by Arab writers. Skillfully, with honesty and sarcasm, he describes life without passing judgment, leaving the reader free to explore, understand, and interact with the narrative. He provides the intimate space for cultural exploration and human engagement that all writers hope to achieve.

THE SELF IN AL-SBOUL'S WORK

Like in the work of most Jordanian writers, Jordan and its culture is strongly present in al-Sboul's language, symbols, characters, conflicts, and description of places. In "You as of Today," the narrative describes the cultural practices and perceptions that govern these practices. Through him, we know what Arabs eat, how they handle conflict, what they say in a religious sermon, how they recruit students to banned political parties, how they resist the state, how they react to war, how they visit prostitutes, how they greet friends, how they attempt suicide, and much more. The self in al-Sboul's work becomes part of the tapestry of the whole. Even when he speaks of others, we see them through his eyes. This willingness to bare his soul forces the readers to become emotionally engaged with the text, regardless if they agree or disagree with the content. The nation and its worries remain central to his inner search. As he looks for himself, he looks into the soul of the nation, trying to understand it and trying to understand himself through it.

As always, there remains a loyal Jordanian. In "Red Indian," for example, the protagonist clearly rejects Western culture and returns home, as proud as a Native American. He explains,

> I walked through the streets of Beirut with my head spinning, feeling an urge
> to go back home. On my way to the travel agency to get a ticket back home,
> I noticed a poultry shop. I stretched my arm through the bars of the cage

that held live chickens and roosters ready to be slaughtered and plucked
a feather from a rooster's tail. It squawked. I stuck the feather in my thick
hair and went on strutting, proud, like a Red Indian.

This reflection on the connection between roots, self, and place is strong
throughout al-Sboul's work. In *Desert Sorrows*, he wrote:

From time before time,
the grains of sand
drank the sorrow in that voice,
entered it in their folds,
returned it to me,
flowing like a dream, magic, melancholy.
As I breathe in its sorrows,
the voice in the folds of my chest
revives my longing for him.
I see him,
a Bedouin with hopeless steps mapped in the desert,
lonely, waiting for traces of dewdrops,
from time before time.[25]

In this poem, al-Sboul sees his steps in the desert as an extension of his
ancestors' journey. He is connected to all that happened to them in the past
but remains lonely, longing, "waiting for traces of dewdrops," for a hope of
a greener future for him and his people.

Women are central in al-Sboul's work. With realism and honesty, he
offers his readers a panoramic view of women in the Arab world and the
taboos, injustices, and circumstances that govern their lives and shape their
relationships with others. Al-Sboul's work and life hold ample evidence of
his respect for women and interest in defending and supporting their rights.
This is especially clear in his poetry. For example, in "What No One Told

Us about Scheherazade" he sees himself as the only one who understands the reality of Scheherazade's plight and the oppression she was subjected to when others failed to do so for centuries.[26] In telling her story, he offers a new, rather progressive narrative.

> My Scheherazade,
>
> My Scheherazade, My friend!
>
> Whatever was said was said.
>
> But you whispered the truth to me:
>
> For a thousand nights,
>
> every night
>
> your only hope was to last through the night.
>
> So when the cock crowed,
>
> announcing to the world the birth of the morning,
>
> you slept with death in your bed.
>
> For a thousand nights,
>
> the light of youth was extinguished from your eyes,
>
> all flavors became the same flavor,
>
> the bitter like the sweet.
>
> After that, it was morning, but was not.
>
> Only the memories of a young girl,
>
> how different from that was Scheherazade!

Al-Sboul considered the subjugation of women part of the general oppression that afflicted his people, and saw himself as the one who understood this oppression and was entrusted with the responsibility of exposing it through his writing. Casually and effortlessly, and with complete transparency, he described these relationships, making them real and haunting at times. He defended women, telling of their suffering and pain, in this poem and many others. Further, he offered his readers an alternative treatment of women in "The Rooster's Cry," introducing a woman who was equal, beautiful, and daring, the man's savior at the breaking point. The male protagonist in the story—a prisoner, just released, confused and broken—found comfort only in the arms of a woman, his friend's wife. Fighting moral and traditional convictions, al-Sboul's protagonist saw her as free, powerful, and gentle at the same time.

In contrast to current mainstream Arab cultural norms, casual sex in al-Sboul's work is not a sin. It is a natural human encounter, the physical and emotional connected, a man and a woman's embrace in a seamless reunion, like "the two halves of a grain of wheat." In "The Rooster's Cry," it is only in this act that the protagonist's trembling soul rests, life becomes complete, and nothing else matters.

Al-Sboul's perception of women is a mixture of the romantic and poetic affection of a Bedouin with progressive socialist views influenced by social forces and loosely bound by culture and tradition. His writings on the subject are bold, direct, and realistic. He does not shy from using erotic images to describe romantic and sexual relationships. Yet, he knows how to use the language to avoid crossing foremost taboos and remain on the edge of the forbidden but still within a safe zone. Al-Sboul skillfully turns the profane to natural, holy, and humane—a union that shakes the human soul, without offending his readers' cultural sensibilities. In "Secret," he wrote:

> When she gestured in consent,
> my veins pulsed with excitement,
> seeing that one I had waited for.
> The journey starts.
> One hand wanders, then rests.
> This evening is gentle.
> The flower pumps inside the vase.
> Silence suffers
> the birth pains of movement.
>
> . . .

The hissing of weaving over her body

repeats its yearning in my ears,

leads the movements of my hands

in the realm of flexibilities.

Colors in the corner, singing with joy,

a carnival of light,

. . .

I pray for you daughter of light

so generous this evening,

so unselfish in giving.

How often I have traveled this distance,

my hand reaping its fruits,

my mouth drinking from its flow.

But I am still thirsty, and my blood is hot

with a mad desire to be spilled in it.

So, listen to this banging

as it gushes strong in my arteries,

longs to live inside you.[27]

As erotic as the images in this poem are, the language remains gentle, carefully selected to provoke the deepest emotions. The sexual encounter is vivid but not vulgar, violent, or demeaning. It displays an equal and balanced relationship, a reflection of al-Sboul's perception of women as equal partners even through the physical act.

This image might be in contrast to the general depiction of Arab men in much of the literature translated into English, but it is common in the work of Arab socialist and progressive writers. It is a testimony of how these writers freed themselves from the bounds and censorship imposed by current social and religious norms and returned to pre- and early periods of Islamic writings, when eroticism in literature was tolerated and even celebrated. This difference between perceived Arab realities in the West and the alternative realities that progressive writers offer highlights the value of translating the works of progressive Arab writers like al-Sboul.

A JOURNEY'S END

In all three texts in this book, and most of the poems in *Desert Sorrows*, pessimism cloaks al-Sboul's writing in a cloud of melancholy, coloring personal experiences and exposing inner feelings and thoughts. It is a reflection of al-Sboul's life itself, where the private merges with the public to create a complex reality in which the boundaries between the two are blurred. He carries not only the weight of the personal defeat he felt after the 1967 War and the stress of daily life, but also the worries of a whole generation that had to live, struggle, endure, and try to understand the trauma. Through all of this, his generation survived, but he did not.

Al-Sboul's endless search for self, true love, a homeland that he could be proud of, and peace by the edge of death exhausted him. Further, events in the Arab world did not end with the 1967 loss but continued to deteriorate. October 1973 brought initial victory, soon followed by a series of negotiations and political maneuverings that al-Sboul saw as surrender and defeat. According to his wife, these and the events that followed comprised an incomprehensible tragedy. He lost hope and felt that he could no longer bring about change. With that, he lost the desire to live, and on November 15, 1973, like many great writers before him, he ended his life.[28]

In his critical essay, Ghalib Halasa sees that the state of the "absurd" that engulfed the world around al-Sboul, changing social norms, and the demagogy of Arab politics produced the disconnected and confused generation that he came to represent. Halasa suggests that these circumstances are what led to al-Sboul's inability to cope with a conflicted and disappointing reality and resulted in his tragic suicide. His suicide remains, to this date, a subject of discussion among his contemporaries and the new generation of Jordanian writers and poets who see his experience as closely tied to their own history and to the destiny of their people.

TRANSLATING AL-SBOUL'S WORK

Tayseer al-Sboul was a skillful prose stylist of the Arabic language. His superb command of words and sentences—precise, rhythmic, intense, and loaded with cultural context—combined with the personal intensity of his experiences produces texts woven in perfect harmony to tell stories that are fully personal, yet steeped in history and tradition. His careful word choice and lucid syntax, along with the cultural, social, and political implications lurking in every corner of his work, is where the challenge in translating his work lies. Translation that focuses only on the functional elements of the text to get the meaning across in English, without careful effort to transfer emotions and thoughts or without positioning events and themes within their cultural milieu and political context strips the narrative of its value and strength.

For a successful translation, the choice of words must be managed in a way that transfers the meaning and context of the original, while maintaining the narrative's flow. I have tried to replicate the elements, spirit, and tone of the Arabic original and still produce a reading that is fluid in English.

In addition to the complexity of linguistic elements in al-Sboul's work, each of the three pieces in this collection posed a unique translation challenge due to the variation in content and style. "You as of Today" is complex, with a fragmented structure tied together by a fine thread linking time, place, events, and perspectives. It is rich in expressions, idioms, poetry, historical references, and semantics that are deeply rooted in religion, politics, and Arab and Jordanian culture. To render the context comprehensible to a Western reader, I found it necessary to include notes that provided contextual information.

In "Red Indian," the author's intentional incorporation of English and French words and expressions to define the orientation of his characters and to explain the protagonist's search for identity posed a unique challenge in translation. To distinguish between the languages used in the narrative, I incorporated subtle references to the language in the dialogue and in a few instances added notes to provide phonological clarification and the social and cultural implications of their use.

In "The Rooster's Cry," the challenge in translation was in the richness of the language, the complexity of the relationships, the intensity of the emotions, and the intimacy of inner dialogue. It was difficult at times to find English words and expressions capable of transferring the wide range of emotions the extensive vocabulary of the Arabic language allows for. Further, al-Sboul's treatment of the complex relationship between the male and female protagonist in the story and his blunt exposure of their inner thoughts and struggles made the translation act itself emotionally charged and intense.

At times, through a close reading while translating the works, I felt as if I were invading the writer's private space, a feeling I also had in translating parts of his other works. I had to be careful not to allow my own knowledge and cultural understanding of the encounters and the characters to inject my own interpretation, which would compromise the accuracy of the translation. I paid very careful attention to reproduce in English the rhythm and breadth of the original dialogue, the imagery in the descriptions, and even the nuanced repetitions that were used to indicate a state of mind or emotion—trying to avoid sacrificing fluency to ensure accuracy while still remaining faithful to the original text.

Intense emotions permeate all of al-Sboul's writings and linger in the mind of the reader long after the encounter with the text. This was the greatest challenge in translating al-Sboul's work. His full attention to detail—including the inner thoughts of his protagonists, and their interactions with people, places, things, and events—make his characters come alive on the pages. His openness in sharing his private life provides the reader access to the private lives of his characters. This empowers the text to engage the reader and tap into common spaces of our shared humanity. The voice of the writer is very loud, passionate, and commanding. This made me even more conscious to transfer that voice, as much as the English language allows, hoping to bring the reader not only the content but also the rich emotions and personal experiences present in the original narrative.

The translated novella and the two stories provide access not only to the heart and mind of an exceptional man but also to the many Arabs he represents. I believe that al-Sboul's work allows readers to step back into history and experience, from a Jordanian perspective, the panorama of events and emotions that shaped, and continue to shape, the minds and hearts of the Arab people.

Al-Sboul turned to history seeking to understand the problems of his time. In return, we should carefully read his work to discover our shared humanity and better understand the realities of the Arab world and the events—influenced by memories, perception, and attitudes that propel what accompanies the social and political changes taking place in the region today.

NOTES

1. See the list of authors that praised al-Sboul's work in A. Y. Majdoubeh, "Taysīr al-Subūl's *You as of Today* in a Postmodernist Context," *Journal of Arabic Literature* 32, no. 3 (2001): 284–301. Also see Habib al-Zyoudi's poem "My Ode Is Missing a Line: To Tayseer al-Sboul," *Al-Rai* newspaper, September 12, 2012.

   See Suliman al-Azrai, *Al-Kalima wal Rasasa: Derasa fe Hayat wa Athar Al-Adeeb Al-Rahel Tayseer Al-Sboul* [The word and the bullet: A study of the life and work of Tayseer Al-Sboul] (Amman, Jordan: Jordanian Ministry of Culture, 2013). Also see *Afkar* 296 (September 2003), which included articles about Tayseer al-Sboul by Majdoleen Abu al-Rub, Suliman al-Azrai, May al-Yateem, Ghalib Halasa, Saud Qubailat, Adi Madanat, Rasmi Abu Ali, Nesreen Akhtarkhavari, and Jafar al-Aqellie.

2. Among other universities, the University of Tafilah, located in the city where al-Sboul was born, holds an annual conference to commemorate al-Sboul's work and passing.

3. A number of singers have performed al-Sboul's poems, including Ghazi Sharqawi, who put to music "Without a Title 2," "The Mariner," and "The Friend of Wind from the Old Man's Eulogy." For an online archive of al-Sboul work, articles, songs, pictures, and studies about him visit http://www.taiseeralsboul. com/novel/.

4. Bahaa Taher, a prominent Egyptian novelist, donated the prize he received from the Jordanian Writers Society to a fund dedicated to the translation of Jordanian works, and he named Tayseer al-Sboul's novella "You as of Today" as the foremost work to be translated.

5. Ahmad Majdoubeh, "Taysīr al-Subūl's *You as of Today,*" *Journal of Arabic Literature* 32(3):284–301.

6. In April 2011, I was asked by the president of the Jordanian Writers Society at the time, Saud Qubailat, and two other members, Samiha Khrais and Huda Fakhori, to translate the novella into English. The Jordanian Writers Society published the translation in 2012. *You as of Today My Homeland* includes an edited version of that translation with additions that were omitted from the original Arabic text and were made available to me by Tayseer's wife, May al-Yateem, in July 2013.

7. Tayseer al-Sboul, *Toi, de's aujourd' hui,* trans. Wael Rabadi (Amman, Jordan: Ministry of Culture, 2012).

8. Tayseer al-Sboul, *Desert Sorrows,* trans. Nesreen Akhtarkhavari and Anthony A. Lee (East Lansing: Michigan State University Press, 2015).

9. See the introduction in al-Sboul, *Desert Sorrows* for further details about the relationship between al-Sboul, Ernest Hemingway, and Vladimir Mayakvousky.

10. May al-Yateem, *Tayseer al-Sboul: al-'Amal al-Kamilah* (Amman, Jordan: Dar Al-Azminah, 1998), 9–12. May al-Yateem—al-Sboul's wife, a physician, and writer—collected and published his work after his death in *Tayseer al-Sboul: al-'Amal al-Kamilah,* hereafter referred to as *al-'Amal al-Kamilah.* All quotes in English, unless otherwise specified, have been translated by Nesreen Akhtarkhavari.

11. Sadiq Abdul al-Haq shared Tayseer's letters to him with Tayseer al-Najar who published them in Taysi al-Najar, "al-Muntaher al-ladhti matazal taskunu miratahu ahzanana al-kubra rasae'l Tayseer al-Sboul. Guswat al-alam hena yakun mahsoos," *Al-Nazwa Magazine* 48 (2009).

12. Shawkat al-Sboul was a leading member in the Jordanian Free Officers

Movement, a group within the Jordanian Army that fought for Jordan's independence from Britain. His affiliation led to his arrest, imprisonment, and exile.

13. Al-Sboul expressed his love for his brother Shawkat in a poem, "The Absent Eagle," in *Desert Sorrows*, 64. The characters of his father, older uncle, and others are also depicted in his poems and stories.

14. "Red Indian" was originally published in *al-'Amal al-Kamilah*.

15. Tayseer al-Sboul, *Ahzan Sahrawiyah* [Desert Sorrows] (Beirut Lebanon: Dar Al-Nahar, 1968).

16. In Ghalib Halasa, "al-Qari' Mubdi'an," http://taiseeralsboul.com; hereafter referred to as Halasa, "al-Qari'." Ghalib Halasa is a highly respected Jordanian novelist and literary critic, and one of the most prolific Arab writers.

17. In July 2013 I interviewed Tayseer's wife, May al-Yateem; his daughter, Saba al-Sboul; his lifelong friend, Adie Medanat; and Suliman al-Azrai, who dedicated much of his academic work to studying Tayseer's life and work.

18. *al-'Amal al-Kamilah*, 10.

19. Ibid.

20. Ibid.

21. Muhammad Obaid Allah, "Tayseer al-Sboul: Al-Musafer ila al-Balad al-Baeed" [Tayseer al-Sboul: The Traveler to a Faraway Land], *Al-Dustor*, November 16, 2007. Also in http://www.taiseeralsboul.com/novel.

22. Halasa, "al-Qari'."

23. Abdallah Redwan, "Derasa fei al-Riwaya al-Urdunieh, Anta Minthu al-Youm— Tayseer al-Sboul: Derasa fei al-Khitab, Derasa fei al-Beya'" [A Study in the Jordanian Novel *You as of Today*, by Tayseer al-Sboul: A Study in Rhetoric and Structure], http://www.taiseeralsboul.com/novel.

24. See for example *Al-Yater* by Hana Mena and *East of the Mediterranean* by Abdul-Rahman Munif.

25. *Desert Sorrows*, 3

26. Ibid., 111, 113.

27. Ibid., 47, 49.

28. See further discussion about his suicide in al-Sboul, *Desert Sorrows*, xxxv–xxxix.

You as of Today

1.

I saw him through the window. He was standing by the kitchen door, holding a stick, looking left, in the direction she entered from. She was white, walked gracefully, and then licked her lips. I was worried that she would come into the living room, so I decided to leave.

Seeing me, he placed his index finger in front of his mouth, and with the other hand holding the stick, ordered me to stay where I was.

He walked toward me. I knew the cat had entered the room and that the ordeal would soon begin. I did not want to watch. So when I heard him slam the door, I ran across the room toward the door. There, the three of us met, and I had no chance of leaving.

The cat cowered in the corner against the wall. He followed her and tried to hit her on the head, but missed and instead hit her back. She rolled over twice and then took off toward the window.

I heard the sound of her claws scratching the glass. She jumped. He hit her again, and this time struck her head. The blood gushed and soiled the floor.

She reached up to the window again, meowing loudly, her claws screeching against the glass. He hit her on the head again. I heard her lungs fill with blood as she tried to breathe. She jerked and lay down, with her cheek to the ground. Her nose bled more, and then she was there, motionless with her eyes still open.

The family sat in the courtyard, between two grapevines that stretched across the opening, waiting for the cannon to sound. I watched the sun fall. The last sliver of the shining disk dove into the western horizon, leaving streak of red flame behind. I saw the muezzin standing on a rock at the top of the mountain. He looked at his watch, and placed it back in his pocket.

My mother passed through the hall carrying a fresh tray of rice, the steam from the tray turned her face red.

I heard her calling me.

"Come and break your fast, Arabi."

The muezzin placed his hand around his mouth and called for prayers: "*Allah-u Akbar! Allah-u Akbar!*"[1]

At that moment, the cannon sounded.[2]

. . .

The meat was cooked in yogurt.[3] My father arranged it over the rice with a stern interest. His small, white beard traced the movement of his dry and pointed face.

I noticed my mother's wrinkles—the skin between her eyes shriveled, carving two deep lines.

All the meat was on the rice.

Not all of it, the shoulder was missing. How could a cat of that size eat that whole chunk? Perhaps she fed it to one of the other cats or maybe to her kittens.

My father tore off his favorite piece, the tongue.

Why did the cat come back? Now, she will have no more meals after that last supper.

"Eat, boy," my father scolded.

"I am not hungry." I left.

. . .

Saber asked, "Are you attending the rally?"

I answered no, and had a feeling that he was not interested in going either.

The evening dawned at the university. In the garden, I saw couples walking. Some were sitting close together on the wooden benches.

"Will you go with me to Abu-Marouf's bar?"

"What about the rally that the Party is having—"[4]

"I am not going."

"Okay. To the bar then."

We walked through the main gate. The yellow leaves covered the sidewalk; the trees were half-naked.

. . .

The next morning, when Arabi opened the door, he saw the cat's decapitated body and her severed head. His stomach churned. He quickly turned his head away and ran to school.

. . .

While the speakers of the Party were busy classifying the enemies of the nation and defining the elements of true Arab unity, he and Saber sat drinking 'Araq at the bar, a small room with poor lighting.[5]

For no particular reason, this bar was Arabi's favorite hangout. Nothing in the place was exceptional. The bartender, Abu-Marouf, never seemed interested in his customers. He served very few appetizers with the drinks and would get annoyed if the customers asked for more, which he did not bother to hide. Still, Arabi liked the place; it met their needs.

. . .

Arabi told Saber about the death of the cat, the Ramadan evenings in the village, and then about his slender, stern father with hawklike eyes.

He talked about his father's tale of the "six daggers" and about the broad leather belt—the one his father folded for greater impact when he used it on his wives.

Arabi saw him use the belt many times. He was not there to witness the tale of the "six daggers" because it happened before his time—during the migration, or "Hajij," when the Ottomans departed—but the storytellers swore that his father was an excellent gunner.

Arabi was wondering who could have mutilated the cat after it was killed by his father. It had to have been dogs or other cats. This might have not seemed important, but it was, considering that the cats could have been her sisters!

Saber said that he understood all that and talked about his "insane" mother, whom they buried at the top of a bare hill. He mentioned that he still thought they should have attended the rally held by the Party.

Arabi told him that he despised listening to political speakers and poets who stomped their feet while reciting political poems, bearing in mind that colonialism, which they were angry about, was not under their feet.

He also said that his mother was sane, but she cried a lot. He added that mothers were all in one of two categories: angry and screaming or humiliated and crying.

Then he added that he remembered an old, secret letter that had a lot written in it. His mind now recalled only a few words: "Bab-al-Wad, bullets whistling, and the roar of bombs."[6]

He knew that it was from his older brother who fought the Jews in the 1948 War.

Arabi said, "After reading the letter, my mother cried nonstop all day long."

• • •

It was summer when Arabi's warrior-brother returned. The food was placed under the trellis covered with grapevines in the courtyard of the house. The whole family sat down for dinner, and the warrior, with his military uniform, was placed at the head of the seating arrangement on the floor. All eyes were focused on him. Even his father seemed distracted from the delicious stuffed grape leaves and squash specially cooked for the occasion.[7] They listened to the battle stories he told with intensity and interest. When the stories reached an exciting climax, they froze and stopped eating, with the food held half way to their mouths, listening in anticipation.

"'Stop shooting.' These were the orders, but I disobeyed them. 'There is no power or will except that of God.' God's will prevailed: we ran out of ammunition."

The warrior's voice filled with anger when he reached the part in the story where he talked about almost being killed.

"May God punish . . ."

A gloomy atmosphere surrounded the circle of diners, as if a long-lost brother had not returned. Arabi decided that since the return of the warrior-brother did not bring any joy, he would not like him.

· · ·

The boy performed his evening prayer and sat with a weight in his heart.

His father's voice came from the courtyard, telling the story of how he got married, which he told time after time. The story bored and embarrassed Arabi.

Arabi read things in the pages of religious textbooks that the Shaikh never taught him. He read that a believer who mentions God in solitude and cries in repentance for fear of God would be rewarded by gaining admittance to heaven.

He performed his prescribed evening prayer. But, sadly, he did not feel like crying. He was sorry that he was not able to complete what was required and lost his chance to be rewarded.

· · ·

Saber asked him about his affair with Aisha.

Arabi said that things were great. She knew when he wanted her and would come up to his room. But he was concerned that this obviously caused her brother pain.

"To hell with the brother!" he added.

He did not actually want him to go to hell. Many of us have sisters and we understand. Arabi did not choose to be his enemy, but he was.

Saber said that all of these were dreadful, oppressive norms. "I have a sister married to a cavalry soldier who is like a mule. He beats her constantly, but she does not want a divorce because of the children. Do you know what I advised her to do?"

"What?"

"To take a lover!"

Arabi thought about what Saber said, not fully believing it. But the story intrigued him anyhow.

· · ·

When he read history, he developed a fondness for the kindhearted historical characters and a hatred of the cruel ones.

Why had they turned against the Imam?[8] He had stood by the entrance of the city gate in the evening, gazing at the sky; his tears flowed over his white beard, and he said,

O world, tempt someone else!
O world, tempt someone else!
Tempt someone else.
I divorce thee thrice.[9]

The problem was that Othman also received the same glad tidings.[10]

• • •

Arabi was quickly recruited to the Party and nervously prepared for enrollment. The teacher himself would perform the ritual. At the appointed time, he was led by an upperclassman to the secret initiation ceremony.

The teacher was waiting under a large walnut tree. Arabi felt embarrassed by his short pants, which did not seem to fit the dignity of the occasion. He listened to the words in praise of his person and other big expressions linking him, with his shorts, to the nation as a whole. He was ready to add more words to the official pledge for greater effect, but a sudden sense of respect stopped him from changing the language. The pledge, after all, was not a game.

The teacher and his fellow student congratulated him. He felt the magnitude of what he had secretly become part of and was overwhelmed by a mysterious, wonderful feeling.

• • •

Holding my neck, my father yelled, "Where is the money?"

"I don't know."

"Oh, you son of a bitch, who did you give it to?"

"Father, I swear by God that I did not take it."

His swift and hard slap fell on my face.

"O father!"

I could not see anymore.

"I did not take it. I swear by God, I did not take it."

He was not leaning over my chest anymore. I saw him hit my mother and heard her scream, so I ran away.

In the evening, it was clear that the matter was a mere mistake in accounting.

"Come and have dinner."

"I do not want any."

"Boy, come and eat."

"I am not hungry . . . I have no appetite."

The night fell heavily.

·   ·   ·

Arabi saw himself sitting on the rooftop, the horizon filled with the red flame of the setting sun. There was silence and then a sudden, strong gust of wind swept the place. He tried to hold on to something but did not find anything. He was thrown off the high rooftop onto the ground, unable to find his own body. He saw a yellow liquid leaking out from somewhere.

"It was me after death . . . and I felt sorry for myself."

"My dreams are so different," said Saber. "They frequently involve incest."

Saber said that he believed in a new morality—that real freedom meant to be beyond fear, free of it, and that fear itself was what should be treated as the actual taboo.

Arabi said that these were very complex issues and that he did not have a conclusive position about them. They ordered another bottle of 'Araq.

2.

In a city with plenty of dust and hot sun—which he later called in his diary *Hajir*, the hottest time of the day, a perfectly befitting name[11]—the warrior grew a belly. He served as a quartermaster, and nobody wanted to execute him anymore.

A unique city at the edge of the desert grew up from refugee camps and barracks. The homes were made of adobe bricks, and the strong Khamaseen—the hot, sandy summer wind—continued to pound the city mercilessly during the summer months. It was a different place: the students were cleaner, and they talked about movies, homeland, books, and political parties with impressive clarity.

· · ·

Arabi informed the comrades that there was a shortage of pamphlets and confided in them that his knowledge and skills in recruiting and leading were lacking. He wanted more information and training. All they did was try to put his mind at ease and praise his interest.

· · ·

The evenings at Hajir were still panting from the midday scorching.

· · ·

The warrior-brother and two soldier friends—Abdu'l-Karim, slender with a spotted face, and Hamad, short and stocky with a thick voice—sprayed the small garden with water. The scent of the wet ground spread. They opened a bottle of 'Araq and poured the drinks. The three soldiers sat on a raised slab of concrete, clinking their cups in toasts and laughing, revealing lists of rations they had stolen.

"You turned to a petty thief, Uncle!"

"Uncle" was just an endearing name they used to call each other.

The "larger" stolen items, as Arabi understood, were fuel and ammunition. The blankets and food products were "small" and the object of their mockery.

"Give us some, 'Abdu'l-Karim!"

The old warrior thought for a moment, then smiled, exposing his stained teeth, and sang with a beautiful voice:

Peace upon thee, O rising moon!
From your eyes swords will loom.
The glory of thy face will rise each day.
And mine will die, and perish soon.[12]

They finished their drinks and kept pouring rounds.

·   ·   ·

A neighbor of the great Imam[13] used to get drunk at night and sing, starting with: "They lost me one day, and what a young lad they lost."[14] The Imam loved to hear his neighbor's voice after saying his evening prayer.

To the contrary, the young leader Abu al-Gasem would recite at the border of China, "No God but God."[15] When the caliph became angry, he ordered that they bring Abu al-Gasem to him, tied over a mule.

Through the wilderness, and during that march of misery and shame, the young leader saw the sun setting and realized that the matter was grave. He whispered to himself:

They lost me, and what a lad they lost!
On a bad day, I was silent after arrest.
Patience, in a struggle with death,
plunged its daggers into my chest.[16]

When he arrived, they brought him before the angry caliph. The caliph ordered that they skin a cow, have the young man placed in the hide, and sew the hide shut. He then ordered them to light a fire and throw the hide, with the young man inside it, into the fire.

At *Hajir*, Abdu'l-Karim sometimes sang the following:

When she returned, she asked about me, and was told,
"No life in him." She clasped her hands, in regret.

·   ·   ·

The broadcasters condemned the ones who they claimed had orchestrated the conspiracies.

They mentioned a large number of people by name, and Arabi believed and agreed that "all of them are rotten." He was pleased every time he heard the broadcaster announce that somewhere in the world, people had slaughtered their rulers. He was not concerned about their heads. Hearing that heads were being lopped off pleased Arabi.

· · ·

Arabi noticed, after a while, that the housekeeper who also served them slept in the corner of the room he slept in. He also noticed that she had a white body, which he saw when the cover slipped off her.

He never thought about her at first. Then he took off her clothes, saw that her body was very clean, so he entered with pleasure. Nevertheless, he became distressed every time he saw her face after she put her clothes on; it was dirty, very dirty.

He said to himself: I would love to have stamped on my body the tattoo of a great nation.[7] I'm sure of that. Then he remembered how the Party's pamphlets bored him. He realized they all said the same thing and decided that there was no need to distribute them weekly. May colonialism fall? Yes, but how? The pamphlets provided no satisfactory answers.

He did not mention this to his comrades. He also did not tell them that he was still carrying on discussions with old, dead historical figures. He knew that something like that would make them laugh. He also did not tell them that his dearest friend was not a member of the Party.

Because the housekeeper continued to have a dirty face, he fell in love from a distance with an olive-skinned girl. He watched her walk to school at the same time every day.

One day he gathered up his courage and tried to give her a love letter. But she apologized and reminded him that people were watching.

· · ·

My mother used to say, "We sprinkle sugar on death." We definitely do. She knew many similar depressing idioms.

I asked my father, "Why, father? Why do you beat her with your wide belt?"

He was in one of his happy moods. He laughed, played with his small white beard, and said, "God damn you, and damn your mother!" Being funny was not one of my father's strong suits. Even when he tried to be funny, he was not. He rolled his eyes at me when he told me that he did not intend to curse me, but his way of being friendly did not please me at all.

The tale of the "six daggers" explained that after being stabbed all over his body with six daggers, my father still walked twenty kilometers. For the sake of his land, he received the six holes in his body. He lay in bed for forty days. Some whispered that he would not live.

One morning, he left his bed and went out to check on the land.

· · ·

A dream:

He was walking in the street, worried about something he had lost. A bus passed by. The seats were full of faces. His mother sat in the last seat. Her face was different—light and pale, like the face of a ghost.

She was dead.

He ran quickly after the bus, but was unable to catch up with it. The pale face turned and looked at him again, as if it was calling him.

He wanted to scream, calling to her. But he discovered that he was without a voice.

A loud sound of honking came from behind him. He looked back and realized that he was delaying traffic, and people were angry, yelling and pointing at him.

He turned to look for the bus, but it had disappeared.

· · ·

The broadcasters continued to yell.

Arabi read plenty of newspapers and poetry. All were angry because of the Nakba.[18] Other than that, he understood little.

He was bored with the housekeeper, but he continued exploring her white body. Then he would discover the filth of her face and become disgusted.

When a girl with a clean face told him that she did not mind him stripping her clothes off, he did, and abandoned the housekeeper. But then he became bored with that girl, too.

He continued to read what the writers, journalists, and politicians wrote about the destiny of the nation. He discovered that so much was written that it could turn the Tigris black for three full days.[19]

After some time, the broadcasters announced that those who had slaughtered the enemies of the people some time earlier were themselves the enemies of the people, and they deserved to have their heads cut off. Arabi thought that was ridiculous.

His interest in their speeches declined because, as with the pamphlets of the Party, they were repetitious and ungrounded.

Arabi grew angry with himself when he discovered that once he grew bored of the naked body of a girl, he lost all desire to touch it.

From time to time, he saw people crowded in the streets, screaming with anger against their leaders, "To hell with the leaders! They are evil."

The soldiers descended to the streets with their steel helmets, their faces painted black.

The people showered the soldiers with stones, and the soldiers showered them with bullets. The condemning banners fell, and the crowds scattered and ran away. Some remained lying on the ground, perhaps dead.

Arabi did not see what actually happened to those lying on the ground, because he ran away, too. At home, they complained about the shortage of bread. Meanwhile, the songs of rebellion streamed through the radio waves condemning the agents of the colonialists, while others condemned the destructive rebels. Then bread and vegetables became available again.

They stopped meeting weekly. "Exceptional circumstances," the comrade-in-charge said. They did not even meet once a month.

Arabi thought it was better that way.

3.

At the plaza, students were running, pulling, kicking, and hitting each other with their hands. A person ran from a far corner and hit another with the trunk of a plant that he had just pulled from the garden. The one being attacked fell, another one fell, and two or three more fell. New groups ran. Screaming and cursing filled the air.

One of the two groups discovered a pile of stones by the corner of the building. They seized them and threw them violently in the direction of the other group. Four fell, their blood gushing on the ground.

The losers fled to the north and climbed the library steps. They shoved each other, trying to escape. A flood of stones fell on them. Then, they all entered the library and closed the glass door. A large number of people ran after them and broke the doors down while yelling and cursing.

Soon they came out, dragging the losers in front of them. One by one, they would beat them at the top of the stairs and then throw them down to the bottom.

Over the walls and through the university gate they ran, trying to escape, but some of them could not climb the wall. Angry students caught them. "You dirty Shoubi, Populist, anti-pan-Arab, foreign nationalist." The students beat them for the third time, perhaps the fourth.

Outside the walls, the police and national security vehicles were waiting to arrest the students who escaped over the walls and to take them "somewhere."

· · ·

The Leader was angry with the Populists, so he announced that they needed to be "taken care of." At the university, the senior comrade told us to be ready to teach the Populists a lesson.

I never liked the senior comrade at the university. He was an idiot, fond of flashing his teeth, thinking that by doing so he gave the impression that he was smiling.

I believed that he liked women more than he liked the nation. When once I was walking with a brown Populist girl, whom I had known for a long time, he called me, flashed his teeth, and said, "Introduce me to her."

"Why, comrade?"

"Forget about that 'comrade' nonsense, and introduce me to her . . . hahaha."

"She is a Populist."

"No problem, my good man. No problem."

I did not introduce him to her, nor did I try to take advantage of her myself.

· · ·

The broadcaster said that the Populists were without morals and that they buried people alive, or murdered them and then hung them on light poles and mutilated them.

The senior comrade explained that the victims of the Populists were members of the Party and would always be its martyrs.

Arabi was not concerned about the martyrs of the Party. It would have been plausible for him not to believe everything the senior comrade said, if it were not for the fact that he had read a poem that said, "We will make ashtrays out of their skulls."

Arabi said that thinking of such ashtrays was much worse than thinking about chopping off the head of a cat.

He convinced himself that he was not interested in an ashtray made out of a skull, whether or not the skull was of a Populist or someone else. In general, he was not fond of skulls.

4.

I left the cafeteria and stopped at the top of the stairs, watching the neon light illuminate the heart of the front garden. The green grass was lit and a belt of darkness surrounded the scene. From beyond the walls, the lights of the street emerged and behind them appeared those of the police station.

I crossed the plaza to the main entrance. I saw part of the police station right across from the entrance, turned left, and went down the street hesitantly. I thought about going to "the place" even though I had left it angry last time.

I could reach it by walking if I turned right. I was not sure I wanted to go. I also did not want to go on foot. That would make the thing even worse.

I passed the museum and walked by the river. I noticed that the traffic was very light. It was too early for night traffic and very late for daytime activities.

I ended up at the taxi station. I had to sit for a long time inside the car waiting for more passengers to come, perhaps because the activities at "the place" had not started yet. Clients usually went there after midnight. Why?

I heard patriotic songs streaming from the radio. I almost changed my mind about going and started to leave the car. I decided not to because I would have been embarrassed to have the driver be disappointed at losing a passenger.

When we arrived at "the place," the company of five passengers, with nothing in common but the goal of the trip, ended. We departed without exchanging a word.

The foul smells of the place penetrated the air and overwhelmed my senses as soon as I entered the outside gate. I first saw the food corner: cookies, fruits, canned food, etc.

My stomach churned. I passed the women on the first floor. They were the cheapest and the dirtiest.

On the second floor, the smell was less intense, and the women were less noisy. They still chewed gum and touched certain parts of their bodies in lewd gestures.

I chose one with the scars of old acne on her face, not one from the crowd that touched certain parts of their bodies.

She told me that she did not want to be completely naked, and why should be none of my business. I did not discuss any further details about the performance with her. She tried to please me by making noises during her act, but I begged her to stop.

Giving me an evil look, she screamed at me, "Do you think you are Don Juan?"

I failed to convince her to accept the money I had planned to pay, not even as a gift. She continued to scream in my face.

At last, I was able to escape, after I left the money at the edge of the sink.

. . .

The next morning, I was taken into the interrogator's room at the General Intelligence Office. A short, ugly man—he seemed to know me, even though I did not recognize him—came and took me from the middle of the university, telling me that I was wanted at the Office.

A handsome man with soft black hair greeted me. He seemed important. He dismissed the ugly man with a nod of his head, and welcomed me, emphasizing that the information he had about me indicated that I was honorable. I was slightly flattered, but the fear of what was coming prevented me from allowing myself to be completely happy.

"Do you know him?"

He handed me a passport, open to the page with the photo. I immediately recognized an old friend, who had been studying medicine in the country where they manufacture ashtrays from skulls.[20]

"Yes. I know him."

"Is he Populist?"

I felt trapped, and all the flattery disappeared.

"Mr. Arabi, hear me well. There is no place for hesitation in cases like this. We are confident of his Populist affiliation. We tortured him, but he did not confess. He is a lowlife Populist. He used you as an alibi, so we know that you knew him. Since the information we have about you is honorable, your testimony will be enough to convict him."

He continued, "The affairs of the nation precede the bounds of friendship. Is he Populist?"

"Yes, he is," I said, hearing my dry voice echo loudly in my head.

He pushed a button, and the ugly man came running and quickly went out to get the Populist. He brought him in. It was clear how much he had been tortured. He did not look anyone in the eye, and he did not know who was in the room.

"You used Mr. Arabi as an alibi?"

Now, the detainee looked up, the muscles of his face quivered when he saw me. Then he dropped his head, agreeing.

"Mr. Arabi, say it in front of him. Is he Populist?"

The time had passed for any equivocation. Arabi heard his voice say: "Yes."

He did not look at his old friend, and no rooster crowed to announce his statement.[21] Instead, an enormous silence engulfed the place.

· · ·

I ran the length of the dark, silent street. I heard the echo of my footsteps stomping at the core of my body. I seemed destined to run, so I ran some more.

Suddenly, at the curve, a military vehicle appeared. The opportunity to avoid it had passed, and I realized that I would definitely be killed. I wanted it to happen quickly, so I threw myself under the wheels and said, "It is done." I heard the sound of my breaking bones. I heard it and waited.

Then, I woke up in the middle of the day.

Arabi went to the university in the morning, and in the evening, drank 'Araq with his writer friends. They all complained about either girls or politics.

· · ·

One writer said, "Brother, the crisis is a crisis of democracy. Israel and colonialism are secondary issues. The crisis is here, inside here. Democracy!"

He took a big bite of a pickle, devoured it quickly, and immediately drank another gulp of 'Araq. "What do you think, Mr. Arabi?"

I was busy looking for a good, fresh nut in the large pile of nuts in front of me, but I did not find any.

"About what?"

"The true nature of the crisis."

I had been thinking that when nuts are stored for a long time, they rot. I searched my head for an answer but could not find one. All the nuts there were rotten, too.

· · ·

In my room on the upper floor, I heard them shouting. The voice of the father and the son were the loudest, and then came the screaming of the mother, followed by a loud bang, apparently on the wooden stairs. I stretched my head through the window and saw the father stomping on his son's stomach. He then reached to his son's mouth as if he was trying to rip it open. The son's mouth was foaming, and his hands were waving in the air aimlessly.

Aisha was also screaming, and the mother was trying to push the yelling father away.

"Let me murder him! Let me murder him!"

I closed the window and pulled myself to my bed. Their screaming quieted down. Then it stopped. I had to wait for a while until Aisha returned to her room to hear the news.

She stood by the door, looking at me with black eyes and long, dark eyelashes, like a she-wolf. She was smiling her daring and sexy smile.

"Come in, Aisha!"

She continued to stare.

"Come in, beautiful. I brought you a chocolate cow."

I pulled out the sweet figure and offered it to her. She smiled, broke off a leg, and started eating it immediately.

"What happened downstairs?"

"'Ali . . . Dad beat him up."

"Why would your father beat up 'Ali?"

She broke the second leg of the cow and started eating it.

"Do you not know?" She smiled.

"No."

"You are the devil," said Aisha.

"How old is 'Ali?"

"Twenty-five years."

"A right age."

"Right for what?"

"For nothing. Tell me: Did your father beat him before I moved in?"

"A lot."

"You used to come up to this room!"

She puckered her lips, pouting.

I then forgot 'Ali and approached her. Her scent raced through my head and filled me with desire.

.   .   .

You are wrong, my friend.

Why do you hate me? It's not my fault. The upper room at the rooftop is what you should hate. I pay extra rent for her . . . This extra rent exhausts my modest monthly allowance. I do have sympathy for you, my friend. At least, I do not think that you should burn in hell.

Why does the matter of her "honor" bother you so much? Have not you, yourself, lost so much more than that? Otherwise, why are you and all the others here, in this city, far away from your home? They have to rent a room; otherwise, how would you be able to attend college, 'Ali?

I understand that Aisha was their daughter, and they expected her to go to the upper room. They did nothing more than collect a few extra liras each month. Besides, she was the kind of girl that would go up there anyway.

You know, you do not have to be miserable over such things.

.   .   .

I used to see them everywhere in Hajir and at the capital here and there. They were everywhere. The few with clean cheeks have not returned. Between the alleys and the tents, their children were always muddy with dirty faces, as if they were birds that had just come out of a chimney.

Always yelling at the entrances of the places that hand out bundles of used clothes, pushing, kicking, ugly old women, young men with unpleasant features, and barefoot children. Even here, where they found a roof over their head and rented a room on the top floor, they were cursing each other.[22] Always finding a reason to curse and scream.

I wondered if the haunting question remained in the skulls they carried on their shoulders: why are they here?

The radio broadcaster confirmed many things about their case. I did not want to hear the views of radio broadcasters. I wanted to ask them, the people. But they were always in turmoil.

Arabi woke to the sound of military music:

Who slaughtered whom? And who wants to rule whom?

His body was exhausted from last night's nightmare. May the devil take all of them away! Soon he will know the real story. He dressed and went down the flight of wooden stairs without shaving his beard. Before he had a chance to wish Um 'Ali[23] "Good Morning," she cried out, announcing, "A coup, Mr. Arabi! May God ruin their lives!"

"A coup? Where?"

"Here, Mr. Arabi. Our lives are ruined, what a shame."

· · ·

Arabi left the house with a desire to know more. Did they do it? Impossible! In the streets, the people gathered around their radios. They were not broadcasting military songs but sweet melodies:

> *Where is the scent and the flowering dream?*
> *Is this your love? How beautiful you seem!*
> *Is this how our meetings will end?*
> *with myrrh and frankincense wafting supreme?*

This was not the time of myrrh and frankincense. Truly, the government officers were not without a sense of humor. He concluded that officers must be fun-loving people. Inspired by the song, his mind paraded the images of a number of beautiful girls he knew.

Then he realized that the song was meant to be patriotic. Beautiful! he thought.

The broadcaster said, "The corrupt dictatorship turned the country into a playground for mercenaries, opportunists, and leeches."

By God, they did it.

The number of soldiers and coup deterrent vehicles were few. Where were the conspirators? What would the Leader do? He was far away.

"Decree number four, launched by . . ."

"Quiet, you and him. Let us listen!"

I saw Saber at the other end of the street, rushing toward me with a red face.

"Saber, Saber!"

He waved his hand and ran toward me with open arms.

"What is this, Saber?"

"Something had to happen."

"But ..."

"I understand. I swear, it had to happen. Are you against it?"

"I don't know."

. . .

A military vehicle passed by. The officer waved to the people, and voices were raised with cheers. Saber waved, greeting him, and Arabi stood watching.

The song was repeated:

Where is the scent and the flowering dream?
Is this your love? How beautiful you seem!

While Arabi was having lunch at the small, crowded, student cafeteria, the radio broadcaster announced that the revolutionaries would negotiate with the Leader to correct past mistakes. "We are not against the Leader, but against his rotten entourage that ruled through corruption."

Some students cheered, while others frowned. Their whispers mixed, "a mockery, they were tricked, etc." In the streets, some people carried a picture of the Leader and marched, saying, "That is what the Leader taught us," and so forth.

Then the broadcaster returned and said that the revolutionaries had changed their minds: that the Leader was, in fact, a dictator and that there was no hope for his reform.

Some of the people were happy, others were miserable, and many stayed silent. Meanwhile, the broadcaster asked the people not to be sad, and he promised a true union among all Arabs.

There were exceptions: Some didn't believe what he said and cried as much as they could. Some became bedridden, and then recuperated after a day or two.

. . .

Some of the elders gathered under a Saqīfah.[24] They publically announced that they were against the Leader (a corrupt dictator) and made the same promise to the people: a true union.

. . .

"May God make this beloved nation prosper . . . and the peace and blessings of God be upon you," the Leader said. His departing words saddened Arabi.

The Khatib, the preacher who delivered the sermon at the university mosque, stopped attacking socialists and atheists, and instead dedicated his sermons to attacking women's short skirts and other related private matters.

"Do not adorn thyself as the women of Jaheliah[25] did in the Days of Ignorance,"[26] he yelled through the microphones.

Praised be God in his Wisdom, Arabi thought. Even the Khatib was now skilled at playing political games and was fully aware of how to be politically correct. Yet, he still managed to have things to attack.

In his imagination, Arabi seated the Imam on the president's chair. At once, the image became fuzzy and confused. The blurriness was a matter of aesthetics, and despite the distortion it caused, the picture was accurate.

Aisha started to change when her family rented another room to a political prisoner.

"It is always cows. Cows, cows, cows," she said when Arabi gave her the sweet figure.

How can I compete with the new politician? he thought. He apologized, explaining to her that the chocolate factory made only chocolate cows. She wanted a deer. He assured her that the factory made only cows.

Things are definitely falling apart, Arabi told himself.

5·

I packed my bag, and at the bottom of the stairs, I saw Um 'Ali and said, "I am sorry I did not tell you earlier, but I am leaving."

"Leaving? Why, neighbor? Did anyone bother you?"

"No, I am just leaving."

Aisha stared at me silently from the kitchen door without smiling. I wanted to leave her with final words, but I was annoyed, and my throat was dry.

"Aisha, did you make him angry?"

She stood there silent, watching me, with no trace of her old tenderness and affection.

"I swear by God, neighbor! No one bothered me. I'm leaving, but I'm not angry."

"Make us two cups of coffee with a little sugar, Aisha. Please, neighbor, drink your coffee and tell me what is wrong."

I wished she would leave me alone.

"I'm leaving because I'm tired, Um 'Ali; and I want no more deals. I'm not lucky. The upper room will no doubt be rented, maybe for more money. It's a considerable rent for me to pay. I wish the price was not that high."

I had to continue swearing that I was not angry. Then I carried my bag, said goodbye to her, and passed by Aisha without saying a word.

· · ·

I went down to the market. Shops of women's clothes, lingerie, and makeup lined both sides of the street.

Election signs were posted on merchandise piled on the sidewalk.

"The voice of Islam under the dome of the parliament: Elect . . ."

"We present to you, the candidate of the workers and farmers, the representative of the proletariat . . ."

"To get rid of colonialism and Zionism, elect . . ."

I remembered Aisha and suddenly realized that I had lost her forever.

I continued to move my gaze between the banners and the shops. Inside me was nothing but emptiness.

· · ·

What did they say to Arabi there?

They said, first we had to trust the Party. The temporary measures taken by the upper leadership were short-term tactics to get us closer to our goals.

"Comrade, did you forget the oppression our Party suffered through? It sacrificed everything for the mission."

"Yes, I remember."

"Do you deny the faults of the dictator?"

"No."

"Then you have to support our position in the matter."

"I don't know. I don't think so . . . no."

"Don't you trust the Party's mission?"

"I don't know."

He was embarrassed and did not explain himself well. He had nothing to explain.

He told them that he personally was not able to serve the Party anymore, and that he would be misleading them if he remained one of them.

"These are unrealistic thoughts, Comrade Arabi. You are honest, and you have never been dishonest in your life."

What was my history with the Party? I did not even beat up the Populists when attacking them was a popular practice. What had I actually contributed to since they baptized me under the large walnut tree?

He did not say that to them. He simply stated that he wished the Party success, and he saw no choice but to resign.

. . .

I told him, "Abu Zohair, I want a room with one bed."

He replied, teasing me, "Every time they evict you from a place, you remember Abu Zohair, huh?"

"They did not evict me this time. I left them."

"A pretty girl?"

"Let us forget about girls. To hell with them! Is the room on the roof occupied?"

"A crazy guy is staying in it. He'll be leaving in a day or two. Sleep on the other bed for two nights."

"And after that, you'll take out the other bed and bring no roommates?"

"Definitely."

We went up the stairs. He introduced me to the man—tan and bold, even though he was still young. He asked, "Where are you from, brother?"

"I'm a Bedouin."

He greeted me warmly. "May the blessings of Allah be upon you. The Bedouins are all noble."

I thanked him and told him that, like others, we are not noble anymore. He interpreted my statement, objecting, and asked, "Now, how are things at the university?"

I told him that everything was fine. He commented, "Since the people deposed the dictator, everything is fine."

We were back to the same boring issues and futile talk. I had no interest in political debate, so I nodded in agreement. Here I was, at the end of the day, on the roof of a three-star hotel with a strange crazy guy invading my space, repeating the same boring story I heard all day.

"The Arabs will discover that the utopian union that the politicians called for is nothing but a trick. Unions take into consideration geographic and racial factors. Is this all that they have to offer! In time, people will realize the importance of the Leader."

I asked, "Which leader?"

He told me I was not thinking clearly, that there was only one person that deserved to be called the Leader and that was the one who was assassinated by the ignorant fools and their lackeys.

He explained to me that the Leader was not a coward, and that he never was scared of death. Further, he informed me that the Leader was killed kneeling. I was surprised, as I was under the impression that people were assassinated while standing.

He explained, "When the Leader was asked if he had a final request, he said, 'Yes!'"

The man waved his arms aimlessly in the air and seemed to be attempting to recall a momentous event from his fractured memory.

"Do you know what the request of the Leader was?"

"Truly, I don't know."

"'Yes,' said the Leader. 'There is a pebble under my knee, remove it.' The soldier bowed meekly and removed it."

"But he is dead now."

"Do ideas die? No. The Leader is the symbol of the only genuine thinker in a crowd of clowns."

He went back to waving his arms and unintentionally looked as if he was shouting at my face. I told him that I had little interest in politics or in any of the leaders.

· · ·

"Here is one bed for a special price. Don't leave us for a house with rooms for rent."

"No more rooms for rent. I want to finish my studies and do my homework. I learn best when studying while pacing on this rooftop."

He reminded me that I had said something to that effect in the past and later changed my mind. He warned me that women and boarding houses would ruin my future, if I were not careful.

· · ·

Arabi suffered from nightmares.

One in particular recurred frequently and added to his physical exhaustion. He would dream that he saw himself going through a mandatory exercise, not for the sake of exercising but purposelessly. His legs were raised in the air while he stood on his head. His legs were light, as if they had no weight. He tried to drop them but failed. His neck hurt, and he said to himself, "I am sleeping, and this is just a nightmare that I need to wake up from."

He always tried to scream, but, time after time, he failed to wake himself up.

· · ·

The people were called in to select their leaders under the dome of the parliament. Those who won were selected from the names on the signs. The Khatib of the mosque at the university won a large number of votes.

"Our beloved nation is a nation of believers. Praise be to God!"

"Yes, Abu Zohair, yes."

University professors became the people's representatives. The essays and speeches that many of them wrote praising the Leader were still printed in the textbooks that Arabi was required to study. He did not care who he should praise, but he needed to know if he was expected to repeat on his exams what they had written in their books in the past or to write the opposite, which they were preaching now.

. . .

Ramadan approached. The evenings carried with them many fond memories loaded with tastes and scents. At the university, the believers on campus roamed with anger in their eyes; examining the cafeteria, the restaurant, and the alcoves, searching for those tempted to drink or eat.

By al-'Asr, verily, man is in loss.[27]

Arabi chose solitude at the hostel, smoking and taking the time he needed to study.[28]

Although he did not witness students pulling shrubs and using them to fight as they did before, he heard that some of the believers on campus had confronted a student who was smoking and beat him.[29] This led to an alliance of the enemies of fasting: those who belonged to the Party with their former rivals, the Populists. Together, they attacked the believers.[30]

It was said that the believers on campus were reinforced by outside groups of believers, who were brought into the sanctuary of the university. On the other hand, some denied this, claiming that the rivals were just cowards.

Regardless of what was said, the new shrubs at the university were pulled out for the second time. The battle ended with the believers sending their nonbeliever enemies beyond the walls of the university and forbidding them to return during the holy month of Ramadan.

The radio broadcasters continued filling the air with their curses, and they exchanged insults—"destructive atheists," "colonial agents," "narrow-minded bigots," etc. "God the Most Great, will prevent the fall of Islam."

Arabi heard all of this in the streets and in restaurants, and he had no choice but to listen.

One dawn, an angry broadcaster said that the representatives of the people in parliament were actually traitors and opportunists and even agents of colonialism, and that they had been sent off to prison. He then added that, since the army came out and exercised its leadership role, power had shifted to the hands of the army and the security forces. The people were elated.

6.

We used to sit at the café in the morning. In the evening, we talked about politics and listened to the broadcasters. Other customers were there as well.

The intelligence officer said, "Your degree turns into a worthless piece of paper as soon as I write two words on it. Do you know what they are?"

I did not answer.

"Two words only, 'Not Approved,' and no government agency or any other institution will employ you. Is this understood?"

"Understood."

"You don't care?"

I told him that I cared very much, but I was not involved in politics. I repeated to him that I quit the Party.

"I understand that. I am not asking you about yourself. I am asking about the active Party members. I want a full list of their names and all the meetings that you know of. I do not want misleading or incomplete information."

I told him that I didn't know the current Party members. "Yes, I used to know them but many things changed, and many of them are not active anymore."

"Do you think that just because you left the country you stopped being under our surveillance? No. Would you like me to tell you the details of your life during the last four years, while you were out of the country?"

I thanked him and informed him that I didn't believe in politics and Parties anymore.

"Now, are you with us or against us?"

I told him that I was not with or against anyone.

"No. If you are not with us, then you are against us. Would you like me to give you details about your illegal meetings and the meetings of the others?" Without waiting for my answer, he added, "I have it. I don't need your help."

The interrogation ended.

I was sure that he had all the details. That was not the issue. He was just like my old Party, his rival: regardless of the animosity between them, they both interfered in my personal affairs, and that bothered me.

· · ·

Young people did not agree on how to solve the Palestinian issue. "It is deep in the heart," proclaimed the broadcaster, but he did not explain further.

They were aware of world opinion—that we appeared to the world as savages, throwing children into the sea.[31] But our focus needed to be on removing the presence of the Israeli aggression. The question was how? They never explained in detail.

The youth were not talking about Palestine all the time. They were playing cards, board games, and chess. They were not satisfied with what was said on the radio, but they did not express their thoughts in any details.

· · ·

It was during this time that my father died.

A rumor spread among the young people in the café that citizen Arabi was writing a novel, so some of their learned ones came to Arabi, stood over his head, and asked him about the truth of the matter.

He was a little embarrassed and told them that he was writing something strange and did not know what to call it.

They questioned him about the reason for writing this thing and asked why he was writing it if he did not know what it was.

He said, "I write it because it bothers me."

They approached him, surrounded him, and quickly inspected his short manuscript.

"Beautiful, beautiful! But didn't you notice that it lacks direction?"

"Yes. This thing has no direction."

"Reexamine what you wrote—you are forcing history into the narrative."

· · ·

Arabi tried to explain to the gentlemen that he never liked to force things. He told them the story of a small bird that went into the opening of the chimney and all of his feathers turned black.

"He was a refugee," Arabi said with a sad smile. "His leg was broken. My mother suggested roasting him for me. I carried him and placed him on a bare tree, to give him some dignity. Do you know, gentlemen, what happened to him next?"

"No."

"A cat crushed him between her teeth."

"A story that could have happened, but . . ."

"A story that happened, sir? What do you mean by 'It could have happened?'"

"Yes, yes, but it has nothing to do with the subject."

"It has. The cat's actions upset me."

· · ·

His mouth was foaming. He was cursing me, cursing her, and waving his hands in the air, screaming, "I took care of you, dog!" He did not hit anyone. He started to but stopped himself.

He stared at me with bulging eyes. "Hypocrite! Say that you want the horse and the rifle."

"I do not want them. I am concerned about the women."

"Who put you in charge of the women, hypocrite?"

We had just returned from the cemetery, where we laid the body of the old man to rest. And there we were, right after that, screaming at each other.

My mother approached from the kitchen and heard our voices, tears streaming down her wrinkled face.

"This is my house. Put it in my name."

"You bitch, how is this house yours?"

She shed more tears and stared into space strangely. I was worried that she was losing her mind.

"You have . . . no fear of God . . . This is my house . . . my inheritance."

She spoke haltingly, like the speech of children when they cry. He cursed her again and left to perform his daily prayers.

My mother kept crying and rambling. I was surprised that she was able to think clearly. She wanted her house.

They would continue to yell at each other for a month, if that was what it would take. To hell with the women, the horse, and the rifle. Trouble comes like "Bab al-Wad and the sound of bullets."[32] Liars and hypocrites.

I told him that he could have the horse and the rifle. His face glowed, and he announced that he would never abuse anyone's rights. He was not a lowlife who took advantage of women. I assured him of my confidence in him, and we agreed to settle the issue of inheritance later. But what was he going to do with the horse?

At that point, I stopped worrying about it and left him to do with it as he pleased.

7.

Things got bad a long time ago.

What do I know? They may have never been good. A noble man was sewn into the hide of a cow, someone who spread the glad tidings, telling people that there is "No God but God"—a strategy that led to victory. Why the hide of a cow? Long ago, a man saw this happen, detested it, and became uninterested in life.

"Kill me," he screamed at them. "You will receive your just rewards, and I will die a martyr."

They turned their faces away with pity. "Madness in his mind," they said.

When they realized that the matter was worse than madness in the mind, they said, "By God, we should kill him," and they did. No problem, no concern.

The Tatar general had a strategy that led to victory. He was actually a little late.

The caliph left, frowning, and handed him the keys. The history books do not mention whether the Tatar general held the chin of the caliph in jest.

We do not think that he did. Further, the General was generous and extended protection to the lives and riches of the people. It is not true what was said about his soldiers throwing the library of the city into the river. It is not true that the water of the river turned black for three full days.

Let us assume that was true. Didn't the river turn clear again after those three days?

"It was only three days."

.   .   .

The soldiers and the refugee crossed the damaged bridge. The soldier did not cross with them. He had been dead for three days. For three days, he was left alone by the bridge, dressed in his official yellow uniform, his heavy shoes still shining, a terrible stench, but his heavy shoes were still shining.

His cheek was touching the ground. I did not see his eyes. They might have been open. I did not see them. When the soldier was alive, he used to come back in the evening carrying potatoes, tomatoes, and onions.

The bridge was hanging over the river but no more potatoes. Noon came, and the soldier was still by the river.

.   .   .

Once, I heard a news broadcaster say, "Get angry, my brother."

.   .   .

That day, Citizen Arabi woke up late as usual. He looked at the things in the room from under his covers. The room was quiet. He was not expected at any job, so he continued focusing his eyes on the things around the room. He felt his legs under the covers, limbs not expected to rise; tasted the bitterness in his mouth produced by smoking; and reminded himself that moving was a matter that required his attention.

He tried to force himself to think about the radio. Ideas flashed though his head. They filled the air with screaming. "Your degree turns into a worthless piece of paper as soon as I write two words on it. Do you know what they are? . . . 'Not Approved.'" It was critical to convince him to drop the "Not." It had been said that there was a new policy regarding sharing personal files. The new people confused this with the big issue and tied it to closer collaboration among Arab countries. It was critical to have new policies.

"We are rotting . . . at this point, things have gotten worse. It seems that they will escalate. What did the Israeli general mean by his threat?[33] He was arrogant and rude, with a strategy of winning."

Damn them!

Arabi stretched his arm and grabbed the radio. The world had turned upside down. (It must have actually happened).

He went to the bathroom with the radio in his hand, unable to stay away from it, not even for a moment. He made his coffee while listening to the sizzling reports of victories and great statistics.

No, I should go out.

. . .

Citizen Arabi took off his pajamas, did not shave his beard, and decided that he should let go of the radio. He would listen to the reports at Hamza's house. Hamza would not be sleeping now. His father always woke him up when important things happened.

He saw the sun glowing and citizens running. Music filled the streets and people were chattering with joy and excitement. By God, it had happened at last!

Hamza greeted him yelling like a Red Indian—not sleeping, more awake than the devil himself. They kissed and sat listening to the reports and the songs.

We exchanged happy and encouraging statements, clapped after each new report, and looked for a map to track some of the land victories. We found only a small one that did not meet our needs.

Then Hamza announced that he could not sit there anymore, and suggested that we go out. I immediately agreed. We crossed the main square, rushing on with the running crowd, while the sound of multiple radio stations filled the air. Hamza suggested that we go to visit our friend Eissa at the Ministry of Information, and I agreed. This time, I thought, my brother will participate in a different war. I was happy that I gave him the horse and the rifle, despite the fact that he sold them.

Eissa met us dancing. We danced with him joyfully, then sat and smoked while we listened to the radio. We even had to send one of the office boys to buy us more cigarettes.

Then the minister called his employees to a general meeting, and Eissa was informed that the role of the media was as important as that of the soldier in the field. He told us that when he returned from the meeting. Hamza became annoyed that the increase in the number associated with Arabs victories was slowing down.

Eissa explained to him that it was not a game, and these victories were very satisfactory.

The voices of the broadcasters grew tired, so their screaming became a little less, but our spirits remained high. I suggested to Hamza that we go out again, and he agreed.

·　·　·

We saw people running to the bakeries. Like them, we pushed our way in and bought extra rations of bread but did not buy any vegetables.

I pointed up at the sky and looked at Hamza.

"Their airplanes or ours?" he asked.

"Their airplanes."

"Impossible!"

Finally, we heard the sound of the siren. The airplanes had started bombing the airport, and we saw clouds of black smoke rise. We heard no noise. We ran quickly, looking for shelter. We entered the reception area of a doctor's office and were crammed in with other citizens. "A mock attack, a drill," explained a man in his forties. When I told him that it was a real attack, he yelled at me angrily and asked me to stop spreading rumors. I stopped.

Then we heard the siren announcing safety and ran out. The airplanes appeared again. We heard the sirens again, but we did not respond this time. The attack was at a great distance, and each of us went home.

8.

When things were over, Citizen Arabi walked through the streets aimlessly, meandering around like a dizzy fly. He watched the military vehicles returning, blotched with mud, and understood that it was camouflage. Most of the vehicles were trucks carrying soldiers, silent and frowning. He rarely saw fighting vehicles. He heard one of the soldiers trying to explain the situation to a taxi driver. "The airplanes, oh God, the airplanes."

Arabi himself had often dreamed about the airplanes. He saw one of the soldiers falling with his parachute over their courtyard. Even though Arabi froze in his place and did nothing, the soldier kicked him in his face with his heavy shoes, and Arabi fell to the ground.

In the following days, people tried to use their heads to understand the turn of events. They talked to each other and to Mr. Arabi about the war and its aftermath.

The broadcaster explained that oil was the central nerve of colonialism and emphasized that it was a great weapon. Arabi tried to understand the relevance of this to the topic at hand, but he could not.

Citizen Arabi did not understand this view.

· · ·

One night, I remained in my room alone.

I have no desire. One says this in our village when he has no desire to eat. I always believed that it meant no desire not only for food but also for a host of other things.

I did not have lunch. I had no desire. Instead, I slept through midday and through a large part of the afternoon.

I had no interest in joining them at the café, and I never wanted to see anyone playing cards or a backgammon game again.

I found something to eat: bread, strained yogurt, and olives. I placed the teapot on the electric burner. It was very slow, but it was all I had.

A grown person asleep, dreaming of daylight.

I tried to distract myself from thinking about that by cleaning the wooden table and making up my bed.

· · ·

The intelligence officer explained to me that there was no intention of revisiting the issue of personal files. He assured me that no one was holding grudges against anyone. "It's just that you can't find a job because half of the country has been lost." He told me that the issue of the files would be resolved in time and assured me that he personally was growing tired of files.

· · ·

From my window, I saw the lights of the city glowing in the distance. I did not like the dusk. It seemed like it was there to help one adjust one's eyes and soul to the night.

· · ·

Maybe he was bored with the files. What difference did they make? The intelligence officer he had talked to, all the other officers, and those like them were living comfortably under those distant lights. They all had homes, good jobs, and wives.

I tried to purge this from my mind.

I picked up a magazine that I had already read and looked at the pictures of the women in it. The dresses were pulled up to their thighs. This did not happen by accident; it was part of a calculated move, part of an orchestrated strategy to seduce.

The important thing is that your plan succeeded.

Q: How could you agree to play a role of a Zionist *Ghaniah*, a loose woman?

A: I accepted this role for my country. First, I was worried about tarnishing my reputation among my beloved fans, and then I went back and said that the fans would understand, etc. He revealed his plans to me, etc.[34]

I threw the magazine aside.

Finally, the tea was ready. I placed the tea and the two cups on the table and pulled a chair to sit. Before I started, a fly landed on the yogurt. With the palm of my hand, I shooed it away; it flew around and landed on the yogurt again.

I saw the kitchen towel. It was not exactly clean, and the idea of using it repulsed me. I wondered if I should I kill it with my shoe.

No.

The miserable fly did not leave me alone, not even at night.

It landed on the table; I hit it with my hand; dead. I moved the food away, leaving the tea.

I smoked a cigarette. "Your degree becomes a worthless paper"—useless. What is there that did not become worthless?

In his dreams, Arabi slept with a girl and discovered she was dead. He almost lost his mind when he discovered that.

In his dreams, he talked to himself, died time after time and came back to life again, and then woke up. Why?

His veteran-brother considered the matter a financial issue and calculated profits and losses. He dragged him into a lengthy process to divide the inheritance, and reached a final distribution. He could convince even the devil himself of his calculation process. He divided the inheritance according to *Sharia* law, subtracted loans and university expenses, and landed Arabi in the negative.

Arabi's account was always in the negative.

The greatest trick would be if death were just a dream—a great trick after all those years of dreaming.

•   •   •

Arabi left his room, walking down toward the city. He could see the lights and the traffic ahead, but he was still far away. Behind the glass stood a heavyset man buying sweets and two young men criticizing a film poster. An unattractive woman crossed the street. Where was she going? Where were they all going?

"Did you ask for two packs, sir?" He looked at me from behind his glasses. "Yes, two packs."

I gave him two silver coins. He gave me back two red coins. I felt their cold metal in my hand.

In his room, he placed the two packs of cigarettes on the table. His mind stopped thinking, but his stomach was empty, churning from lack of food and excessive smoking. The bitter taste lingered in his dry mouth.

Under the bed, he could see part of his suitcase covered with dust. The door of the small closet was open, and over its edge hung another pair of trousers. The dust was on the floor and everywhere he looked.

He took a number of pills out of a paper tube and stacked them on the magazine. He got up and filled a half-cup of water, dropped the pills in, and stirred.

The small particles moved in a circular motion and crashed at the inner edges of the cup. He stopped stirring, and the particles quickly sank to the bottom.

He was not in a hurry. He placed the cup on the floor and sat on the bed, smoking and watching the white layer settle at the bottom of the cup. He had no previous experience with this, so he continued to watch.

In his mind, he wanted to drink the liquid all at once. He stirred it, saw the rushing particles slam into the glass, and picked it up.

His stomach knotted up, and he felt the weight of a rock on his chest. His hand became completely stiff, as it often did in his dreams.

•   •   •

I felt a strong desire to hear something, anything. I picked up the radio, and I noticed my hand tremble. I turned it on and tossed it on the bed.

Even the evening prayer was now accompanied by sad melodies streaming from a wooden flute somewhere!

This was not music. It was something different: the breath of man through a hollow reed, not to bring pleasure, but to stick something sharp into the heart.

My mother frequently repeated the story of my birth. She told me that she left me crying for a whole week after my birth, without taking care of me, and that our old neighbor cared for me and nourished me with anise tea. Otherwise, there would not have been an Arabi!

At that time, my father had not returned from his pilgrimage to Mecca, according to schedule, with the other pilgrims. It was said that he had lost his way and had been killed. My mother was mourning him, and she had no interest in a child.

(I always felt that was unkind, just like skinning skulls.)[35]

Allah-u Akbar, Allah-u Akbar.

"Welcomed is the mention of God," my mother used to say whenever she heard the call to prayer.

She used to repeat, "Definitely a day will come when this sad one will be happy." But I had never seen her happy.

· · ·

Arabi put out his cigarette on the floor of the room and then got up, picked up the glass, and walked with it to the sink where he poured it out and ran the faucet.

He returned and lay down on his bed.

"A great man traveled to many countries of the world and saw a great number of catastrophes. But he had never seen a whole nation drown in sadness like my people." That is what he openly announced.

9.

On June 10, the final day of the 1967 War, I went down to the Jordan River to see what had happened to my country. I saw destroyed and burned out army vehicles all along the way. Before I reached the river, I saw a dead mule on the side of the road; it was bloated and ready to explode.

Then I saw the wrecked bridge, and I saw people from different walks of society in turmoil. Now, I remember nothing of that place except that there was aimless movement and mangled voices. I cannot see now what could have possibly been accomplished by being there at that point.

The bridge was terribly damaged, but parts of it were still hanging together. There was a woman there trying to cross, climbing the wreckage, and holding on to what used to be the rail of the bridge. She was very much afraid of falling but went on trying to cross. I still remember her small face. Even though I had always heard about the paleness of scared faces, I had never seen other faces like it—small and as yellow as a dried peel of a lemon. People were watching her in desperation and then moving away.

I stood at the last standing point on the bridge. Now, I realize that I was looking for the last inch of what remained from my homeland. I intentionally stood there at that last section, holding on.

I saw the river, and I saw the distant high peaks of the mountains. I did not see soldiers. I looked for them. I was sure that they could see me, but I could not see them.

I looked through the broken bridge without paying attention to the people around me. I saw the land with its scorching scent. I had often crossed this bridge to the other bank. My mind was consumed by small details: a thorny bush, an ordinary stone. I intentionally looked for them.

I then noticed that the whole scene was really bothering me. A foul odor reached me, but I could not locate where it was coming from. After that, I moved back and stood alone at the far right corner of the falling bridge.

The odor intensified. I desperately looked for its source. I saw a woven sieve, and under it lay the body of a dead soldier in full uniform.

On the way back, the night fell while we drove up the mountain. We were not saying much, just a few infrequent, fragmented words. This might have been because of the nature of the place or perhaps because it was nighttime or for some other reason I was not aware of. The words were echoing, making it seem as if we were hearing double. I have never seen a night like that. Something in it made it resemble the way I imagined the last night in the life of the human race.

· · ·

I tried to look at the matter from my own perspective, but I still could not understand. I loudly said, "Defeat. That is what it is." But I still could not wrap my mind around it. It was not just a defeat; it was something else, much more.

Once, I saw in the middle of the road a cat hit by a car, blood coming out of her ear and the side of her face. She was running in a circle no more than one meter in size, her eyes in a fixed position, and she constantly moved. I did not know what she was staring at or what she wanted. Now, I understood how she felt.

Radios were everywhere. I did not understand why our broadcasters should still be speaking. It appeared to me that the matter was a simple question that needed an answer: are we people, or are we punching bags stuffed with hay, used by boxers from the time of Hulagu, when the Mongol conquered us? And now, we are conquered again by this general.[36]

What do they call them? Defense Forces? Defending what?

Even with this title, they stomped on us. What a mockery—cover-ups and lies! Everything that had been said in relation to this war was just cover-ups and lies from all sides. I wanted neither to see it nor to hear it.

There were months of freedom in the name of the "Dark Ages." I am referring to what was in a particular skull, my skull. I believe that it was a very personal matter. My case was the case of a citizen with a perpetual desire to bare on my soul the tattoo, the stamp, of a strong nation. It was impossible for me to accept any compromises. Now, I wondered, was this a nation or a hay-stuffed punching bag?

· · ·

The general nestled comfortably inside my skull. Here he had the ability to loosen the patch on his eye, stretch his legs, and rest—not at his home and not in his military quarters, turned to a museum decorated with scenes of glorious victory, but inside a skull, my skull. The general had the uncanny ability to stare at his patched eye and conclude that being with one blind eye was the norm; and there was no voice in that skull that would argue with him.

· · ·

For an old sage who traveled the world and was exposed to all the injustice and catastrophes of history, he confessed that he never came across a nation drowning in sadness like my nation. It was obvious that the nation had turned into one creature—huge, wounded, stumbling, and slowly falling. There was no shock greater than that.

And at the final scene, may peace, blessings, and the bounties of God fall upon you.

· · ·

For thousands of years, Arabi had not cried. He made it through all of the injustices of history and its catastrophes, one after another. Isolated, trivial, they all passed, and Arabi did not cry.

The farmers left their villages. The homemakers came out with nightgowns; men and children, some without shoes, all came out. The lights were off. Their numbers started to increase, they were screaming louder, and then they broke into a crying fit.

What happened to him?

In one second, his imagination was washed clean of all images. He was instantly devoid of imagining the injustices in his history. Yet, despite that, they were all still there. More than a thousand times, this body, which he as part of was attacked. Many nations trampled over it and kicked it. Arabi was not crying over a particular regime. He did not know why he was crying.

He buried his head in his pillow and began to weep. He heard his own voice breaking and cracking, worse than any injured cat. That scared him, and he became lost in a full fit of weeping. He started to cry loudly, and his voice was not shivering anymore; it was more like a scream of a wounded being.[37] He held tight to his bedding, afraid that there would be nothing left to hold to; then he held tighter and cried more. Everything vanished from his mind, except being there on his bed. It was nighttime. He gathered within himself all the injustices of the past. At the sound of his weeping, he wept even more.

Then, it was time for all of that to end, as every other tragedy ends. My people might be just as stupid as their opponents liked to paint them; or it could be that they were shocked into it when they were being beaten, thinking that it was odd for it to be happening and that the whole thing was implausible. It could further be strictly personal—about an individual who looked within himself in an attempt to understand his place in history.

Our teacher used to explain the story of Europe as if he were watching the events take place. He used to call the period between the fifth and the ninth centuries A.D. the "Dark Ages." The two words had a strange ring to them. I believed that this was a matter of pride.[38] The full gambit of human pride was present in these two words. When five complete centuries were ridiculed and reduced to two meager words, "Dark Ages," they were forced to think intentionally or unconsciously about light.

"Dark Ages" means that there was a light that was extinguished for five hundred years, then it was lit again, and for that, they were proud.

· · ·

(Why should I care about them?)

· · ·

Who was the general talking about—about my people and me? Who asked him to worry about our affairs? I saw pride in his eyes, but I had no respect for him. I had seen my people in the desert, the thirsty soldiers, wandering aimlessly. It was summer; I saw the general's men waving water in front of the soldiers, then hiding it and laughing. I saw my people falling, spreading their arms on the hot sand, tormented by a sweet love for their homeland. Nothing was larger than that except the bitter bleakness that anguished my soul and the souls of my people throughout the long months of darkness.

The issue was not only that I saw the general small like a fly, but that I saw him dirty like a fly. The question was never whether this nation was a nation of fighters or not.

They fought better than they did in '56, the general graciously admitted.[39]

The problem was that this nation was forced to fight. Therefore, the strange echo remained. As the history teacher said to the children, "The period stretching between the fifth and ninth centuries A.D. is the period known as the 'Dark Ages.'"

NOTES

1. The first words in the Muslim call to prayer, this phrase literally means, "God is Greater, God is Greater." The call to prayer at sunset during Ramadan, the Muslim month of fasting, announces the end of the fast for the day.

2. In some regions of the Arab world, a cannon is sounded to announce *iftar* (the meal that breaks the fast) at sunset during Ramadan.

3. *Mansaf* is a traditional Jordanian dish made of lamb cooked with diluted dried yogurt and spread over a layer of thin bread covered with a bed of rice. When cooked on special occasions—such as weddings, funerals, and family gatherings—the pieces of a whole lamb are placed over the rice with the head in the middle.

4. The party referred to here is the Ba'ath Party.

5. *'Araq* is a distilled, colorless, alcoholic beverage often flavored with anise and commonly produced in the Levant and other Middle Eastern countries.

6. Bab al-wad was the location of a fierce battle that Jordan's Arab Legion won during the 1948 War.

7. The food served was *mahashi,* stuffed grape leaves and squash. It is served as a special meal at family gatherings in the Levant.

8. Imam 'Ali bin abi Talib, the fourth caliph, was the first cousin and close companion of the Prophet Muhammad.

9.   Imam 'Ali's statement, "O world, tempt someone else. . . . I divorce thee thrice," demonstrates his detachment from the material world. According to Islamic law, a triple divorce signals a final divorce, after which a man cannot remarry his divorced wife unless she marries another man, consummates the marriage, and is then divorced by that man.

10.   Othman bin Affan was the third caliph. Othman was selected by a group of six close companions of the Prophet who were appointed by Omar ibn al-Khattab, the second caliph, to consult and choose a successor. The choice was between 'Ali and Othman. Some believe that 'Ali was supposed to be appointed caliph prior to Othman, and even before the other two caliphs. Othman's appointment and the subsequent assassination of 'Ali became the basis of much internal conflict in Islam and ultimately led to the division between Shi'i and Sunni Muslims.

11.   Hajir is noon time, when the sun is very hot, especially in the desert.

12.   This poem by Kamal al-Din ibn al-Nabeh (1164–1222)—who lived during the reign of the Ayyubid Dynasty and wrote poetry praising its caliphs—gained additional popularity when it was used as the lyric of a song performed by the legendary twentieth-century Egyptian singer Oum Kalthoum.

13.   Imam Abu-Hanifa was one of the four main Sunni Imams.

14.   This line comes from a poem by Abdullah bin Omar bin A'mr bin Othman bin Affan (the grandson of the third caliph). He was put in prison for his promiscuous lifestyle and poetry. The lines are part of a poem, written in prison, in which he praises himself and promises to reward the caliph by praising him with beautiful poetry if he is set free.

15.   Muhammad Abu al-Qasim al-Thaqafi was appointed by the Umayyad caliph, al-Walid ibn 'Abdul-Malik. The youngest Muslim caliph, Abu al-Qasim led the Islamic expansion to China and East Asia at the age of seventeen. He was deposed and ordered to return to Iraq by the next caliph, Sulayman ibn 'Abd al-Malik, because of his relationship with al-Hajjaj, the former governor of Basra, whom the new caliph despised. Upon his return, Abu al-Qasim was captured, imprisoned, tortured for months, and then killed.

16.   These verses are part of a famous poem about love and regret. The source is disputed. Some say that it was written by Yazid, the son of the Umayyad caliph Muawiyah, while others say that it was written by a Syrian poet, Muhammad ibn Ahmad al-Adnani al-Dimashqi, or al-Wa'Wa' al-Dimashgi.

17. The author uses the word *washm*, which refers to a traditional tattooing used by Arabs in the past as a beauty mark or to indicate affiliation.

18. The *Nakba*—or *al-Nakba*, "the Catastrophe"—refers to the 1948 Arab-Israeli War (after May 15, 1948), which involved military forces from Palestine, Iraq, Transjordan, Syria, and Egypt against the Israeli military forces. The Arabs lost the war, which marked the end of the British mandate in Palestine and the establishment of the State of Israel.

19. This refers to the capture of the city by Hulagu, the grandson of Genghis Khan, toward the end of 1257 (during the rule of the Abbasid Caliph al-Musta'sim). Hulagu advanced toward the Abbasid capital with hundreds of thousands of cavalrymen. It was said that they destroyed the city's Grand Library and sacked its invaluable contents, throwing the books in the Tigris, which turned black from the ink for three days.

20. The author is referring to Russia, where many Arab students associated with leftist parties, especially the Communist party, were sent to study and be trained in ideology.

21. This is a reference to the New Testament story of Peter, who denied Christ thrice before the rooster crowed. The story is present in all four gospels.

22. The passage "ugly old women, young men with unpleasant features, and barefoot children. Even here, where they found a roof over their head and rented a room on the top floor, they were cursing each other" was added to the text by Dr. May al-Yateem, Tayeer's wife, who indicated that the insert was in the original novel and was accidently dropped from the printed copy.

23. *Um*, Arabic for mother, is used as a title for married women with children. The mother is called by the name of her first son preceded by the title *Um*. If the woman has no sons, the name of her first daughter is used until she bears a son.

24. *Al-saqīfah* is a roof made of palm branches and refers to *Saqīfah banī Sāʿidat*, where the companions of the Prophet gathered after his death to decide on his successor.

25. The term *Jaheliah* refers to the pre-Islamic period in Arabia. Derived from the word *jahl*, which literally means "ignorance," it is known as the Age of Ignorance.

26. The phrase is a quote from Quran 33:33, addressing women, "do not display yourselves as [was] the display of the former times of ignorance."

27. The word *al-`Asr* literally means "afternoon" but is used here in reference to a short sura of the Quran with that title that states, "By al-`Asr, verily, man is in loss, except those who believe and do righteous deeds, and guide one another to truth (good deeds), and recommend to one another to practice patience."

28. Smoking, just like eating and drinking, is forbidden during the daylight hours of Ramadan.

29. The "believers" refers to The Society of Muslim Brothers and their supporters.

30. The "enemies of fasting" refers to members of Al-Ba'th Party (al-Sboul's party) and the Communists, which were derogatively called Populists.

31. At the beginning of the 1967 War, Jamal Abdul-Nasser called on the "fish of the sea" to be ready to devour the Arabs' enemies.

32. The battle at Bab al-Wad—which took place during the 1948 Palestinian-Israeli War near Jerusalem—was fierce, with bullets flying. It was won by Arab troops led by the Jordanian general, Habis al-Majali, and is a point of pride in Jordanian history, an indication that bad situations can end well.

33. General Moshe Dayan, head of the Israeli forces during the 1967 War, led Israeli forces in previous military encounters with Arab armies.

34. A number of stories circulated during that period about the role of the Israeli intelligence in recruiting Arabs as spies. One story in particular concerned a woman who helped expose an Arab Egyptian accused of spying for Israel.

35. From the original manuscript, provided by May al-Yateem.

36. The Israeli general, Moshe Dayan, wore a patch on one of his eyes, the result of an old war injury.

37. The passage "He started to cry loudly, and his voice was not shivering anymore; it was more like a scream of a wounded being" was re-added from the original manuscript, provided by May al-Yateem.

38. The passage "The two words had a strange ring to them. I believed that this was a matter of pride" was re-added from the original manuscript, provided by May al-Yateem.

39. The passage "They fought better than they did in '56, the general graciously admitted" was re-added from the original manuscript, provided by May al-Yateem.

Red Indian

I am a reckless young man, easy to excite. I like women, especially white ones. When I was a child, I used to pet white cats and give speeches to the snow. If a black donkey or a red dog passed by, woe to it!

My father was a committed feudalist. He often left the fields and took me with him to the capital city, where we did nothing but go to the movies to watch Red Indian films. What a ruckus we made when the Indians would tie up the white woman and prepare a big pot to cook her in. I would boo and hiss and make all kind of noises. Father would wave the hem of his *abaya* in excitement and support for the white hero who always rushed to the rescue.

"Yes! O brave one!" my father would yell. "Hurray! A true daring and honorable hero!"

Meanwhile the "hero" would shoot the Indians one after the other.

"Shame on you! Shame on you!" My father would condemn the Indians.

The people in the theater would keep their distance, but my father did not care. When we left the theater, he would swear that he would have me married, if God prolonged his life, to a white American woman. When the excitement overwhelmed him, he would promise me four American wives all at once.

What a grand time I had in the company of my playful father, but destiny was awaiting me. He died suddenly just before his hundredth birthday. I became an orphan, alone, with nothing but few thousand hectares of land and a dream that continued to haunt me. I quickly sold the land, and as was customary, I placed an obituary in the newspaper under the following cliché: "A Flower Withered." As customary also, I added, "A hundred years spent in piety and good deeds prior to leaving us joyfully to reside in the Gardens of Paradise." Then I packed my things and headed to Beirut, looking forward to the dream of having white American wives. I was told that there were plenty of white American women in Beirut.

Blessed be the creator of Beirut and the women of Beirut! By God, milk stands shy before the whiteness of their skin. Beirut, the city of plenty, pleasure, and women in short dresses, where fantasies grow and dreams come true. My mind committed all sorts of sins, with no one or nothing keeping it at bay.

Excellent people, white people, I said to myself. But I cannot understand them. That's my problem and not theirs. How stupid I am. How did I think I could marry Americans without knowing an American word?

So, I set aside a few hours from going to the movies and staring at women to attend the Language Center. Those dreadful times suffocated my free spirit eager to roam the city of Beirut.

After much effort, the professor said to me, "Monsieur, don't bother. You will never learn a foreign language."

Disappointed, I left the Language Center with a simple list of vocabulary the professor said I should continue to study, on the chance they might stick in my brain and help me in my quest. He wished me a happy marriage.

At this critical point of my journey, I met Dr. Muhammad Smith. Of course, this happened in a movie theater. The movie was not about Red Indians; it was about yellow Koreans. It didn't matter. Out of habit, I had the same reaction. With the same enthusiasm, I rooted for the Americans and cursed the Koreans whenever they ambushed or almost captured the white American officer.

In keeping with my father's legacy, I continued to make primitive noises, waving, swearing, warning, and threatening the Koreans in the movie. Apparently, in the heat of my excitement, I hit the man next to me in the eye.

He said, "Monsieur, could you calm down?"

I yelled angrily, "Monsieur, are you a yellow Korean?"

He said in a soft tone, "Pardon monsieur! No. You are impossible!"

What a close friendship develops after a fight. I left the movie theater holding his white wife's arm. She did not stop chirping something I could not understand, but I nodded my head in agreement.

"Oui, madame. Yes . . . yes . . . yes."

Dr. Muhammad informed me after we sat down at a café in al-Roshah, the beautiful Western part of Beirut, that he was a professor of anthropology at the American University of Beirut. Not understanding what he said, I asked, "What does this mean, professor?"

"Oh!"

I remembered and said in English, covering my embarrassment for not initially understanding, "Yes, yes, yes."

His wife asked me, "Monsieur is from where?"

I understood this and responded in English, "From Jordan."

"Oh, Jordan."

"Well, Muhammad . . . refugee . . ." She told her husband something in English while patting my cheeks as if I was a beloved dog.

"Oh, yes, Jordanians are brave."

Dr. Muhammad continued to shake his fist enthusiastically; accidently hitting the waiter who appeared carrying loads of kabob and delicious appetizers. We laughed and the waiter laughed. We were all happy.

When I poured the second cup of *'Araq* down my throat, I felt the usual numbness, and my eyes started to wander through Mrs. Smith's dress. White! White, but she belonged to someone else. It was about time for me to find my own wives and return home.

"Oh, there is Vera . . ." Dr. Muhammad interrupted my contemplation and added, "and Hanan."¹

Mrs. Smith waved, while chirping in English. "Join us."

What a predicament you are in, man! I thought. The orange pants are also fantastic. Everything the women wear in Beirut is great. By God, it is so hard to choose between the two of them. Let it be both then. A green miniskirt and orange pants is what I need.

"Happy to see you," Vera said in English.

Examining her pants and practicing my English, I said, "Happy to see you."
I then added, slipping my sight under Hanan's miniskirt, "Happy to meet you."

Dr. Muhammad introduced me. "Mr. 'Ali from Jordan."[2]

I swear by God that the way he pronounced my name with the soft "a" was more pleasant sounding than its proper guttural pronunciation.

The two birds chirped that they were delighted to have me around. We all sat, happy, talking and drinking more 'Araq.

"Liberty!" Dr. Muhammad yelled in English.

"This is the thing of the day, and all other views and thoughts are empty words," I said.

The conversation moved between Arabic, English, and French.

"Oui. Oui."

I answered and ate another spoon of *kibbeh* that Mrs. Smith offered me.[3]

"Then the Monsieur is from Jordan?" the orange Vera asked.

"Oui, mademoiselle . . . yes."

I answered, mixing English and French, and wished that the professor from the Language Center could see my speedy progress in speaking both languages.

"Oh, poor thing," said the green Ḥanan in English.

"Oui, mademoiselle. Oui," I replied.

"Jordan! What a pity . . . attacks and so many bombs," said Mrs. Smith, mixing English and Arabic.

I understood what she said only because my mother used to call bombs *bumba*, and repeated, mixing the two languages, "Yes, yes, and so many bombs."

I took a large gulp of 'Araq, choked, and started coughing and spitting up. I felt as if my soul was about to leave my body, but the white people came to the rescue.

"Use 'Kleenex,'" said Vera.

"'Fine' is better," said Ḥanan.

"Gentlemen prefer 'Fine,'" said Mrs. Smith.

"Nothing but the best: 'Tembo,'" said Dr. Muhammad.

Their hands stretched out toward me with colored tissues. Tears were flowing from my eyes. I was fighting to keep my soul in my body. Finally, it stopped. I sat amidst their giggles and laughs. I did not like their pitiful laughs and started to feel suspicious of their intentions.

The women continued feeding me *kibbeh*, patting my body and repeating in English, "Poor thing. What a pity!"

I didn't understanding what they meant exactly. I coiled in like a sad porcupine, listening to their laughs and fixing my appearance.

"But all Jordanians are brave," said Vera.

"Of course. All Bedouins are brave," said Ḥanan.

Dr. Muhammad's eyes twinkled, and he said, "Jordanians are guerillas."

I lost my mind when I heard him calling my people and me gorillas. I rose up, fuming, and screamed.

"You are misunderstanding, *guerrillas* in American means—" the doctor tried to explain.

I interrupted him. "Silence, doctor! Don't you ever call us gorillas."

"Crazy, savage," the women whimpered in English and French while staring at my hand.

I had forgotten that I was carrying a knife. It crossed my mind at that point to cook them all in a large pot like Red Indians did in the movies.

"Silence, women! You and her and her and him. Silence, or—"

I threw the knife, and it penetrated the wooden table. The white people scrambled chaotically. I stared angrily at Dr. Muhammad, ready to cook him and his women in one pot. But he escaped, running. I was fully bloated and annoyed, so I decided to leave them alone.

While I was leaving the place, feeling light, my father appeared, smiling. "Life is a stage, my son, a stage!"

"And I am a Red Indian, my father," I said to him.

"You are an empty head with no brain, exactly like your mother," he said to me.

I asked him casually, "Are you having a good time where you are?"

He answered, "It is very hot there, but I am having fun."

"What a miserable ending, old Shaikh! What happened to your beard?"

"They burned it off as a punishment for a false obituary placed in the newspaper about my good deeds and pious life. Damn you and your newspapers! Who put you up to writing such nonsense?"

"They are all like that. It is not my fault."

"Here, our beards are burned off for such lies. Our punishments are doubled with false claims about our lives on earth. Let the people on earth know this."

"I will, I will. Tell me, what is happening with you?"

"I will marry." He waved to me, smiling.

"Even in hell! Who is the unfortunate one?" I asked surprised.

"Her name is Marilyn Molroe."

"Monroe, you ignorant old Shaikh. Monroe, not Molroe."

"Strange," said the old man. As a habit, he reached to hold his beard, and remembered with dismay that it was not there anymore.

"What's strange?" I asked.

"We have an annoying person here who thinks that he is the president of the United States, and his name is Monroe. He is seeking the presidency of hell. He will defeat the devils here. Tell me, is he her father?" the old man asked and winked.

"I don't know. I do not follow American politics. What is it with you? You always find yourself entangled with the Americans."

"I like them. They are kind and white, very white."

I said to him, "You are all damned. You are good for each other. I am a Red Indian. A Red Indian!"

"You are an empty head with no brain, like your mother," the old man repeated his statement over and over again, then winked and said, "The world is a stage. Bye-bye."

"And peace be upon you, silly old Shaikh. Have fun."

I walked through the streets of Beirut with my head spinning, feeling an urge to go back home. On my way to the travel agency to get a ticket back home, I noticed a poultry shop. I stretched my arm through the bars of the cage that held live chickens and roosters ready to be slaughtered and plucked a feather from a rooster's tail. It squawked. I stuck the feather in my thick hair and went on strutting, proud, like a Red Indian.

NOTES

1. Since Dr. Smith could not pronounce the letter $ḥ$, the first letter in the name sounded like h instead.
2. Dr. Muhammad replaced the guttural Arabic letter 'ayn in 'Ali with a soft a, because as a non-native speaker he was unable to pronounce the guttural "'ayn." This technique was used throughout the story on this and other words to highlight the differences in the identities of the speakers.
3. *Kibbeh Nayeh* is a famous dish in the Levant, made of raw meat, onions, bugler wheat and spices.

The Rooster's Cry

1.

In the last minutes of daylight, the door opened, and the prisoner was set free. He was a skinny, disheveled man with a small frame. He walked with slow steps, examining everything around him. He did not feel comfortable with the gloominess that masked the face of the sky. The grayness hindered him from seeing things clearly. He lowered his gaze and turned his sight back to the small shrubs lining his path. They cast long, faded shadows on the place. The whole scene seemed surreal, like a gloomy painting. He walked faster; the light cloth bag hanging from his shoulder brushed against him. He felt it scraping his left thigh. It was almost empty; he realized that it was useless dead weight.

Soon he would be smoking a rolled cigarette with Othman. Even this, he was not in a hurry to do. Gradually, he started getting accustomed to the outside scene. He heard the traffic noise. The sound of a cry far away slowly approached the fence separating the world beyond the prison walls. He gazed at the blurred images in the distance and kept walking.

Othman smiled, waving his arm. Meanwhile, the sun started its descent behind the high castle in the distance. Late in the evening is not the best time to release a prisoner, he thought. He shook the idea out of his head and picked up his pace as he walked toward the outside gate. Othman embraced him warmly. Listening to the smacking noise of the kisses and Othman's voice repeatedly saying, "Thank God you are safe," while crushing him in an animated embrace made him laugh nervously. The prisoner noticed the row of shops to his right, lightbulbs dangling above arranged heaps of vegetables and fruits. To his left, the sun had sunk completely below the horizon.

Othman was short, obese, and wore a dark suit and a bright white shirt. The prisoner did not care for his appearance. They were old friends who had shared a prison cell. He wondered why he felt tense; there was no reason for that.

Othman handed him a cigarette and said, "How badly does a smoker just released from prison need a smoke?"

"Yes, yes," said the prisoner.

He inhaled repeatedly and let out a cloud of smoke and thought: Othman is shorter than I remember him. Maybe he seems so because he gained a lot of weight. His eyebrows are thicker than I remember.

Othman said, pointing to the street, "This is my car. You will have one with time."

The prisoner got in the car, and Othman closed the door. The lights at the market were bright. He thought: Those can almost make you forget the presence of darkness. But when he turned his gaze to the mountains, which were full of houses lit with tiny lightbulbs, it seemed to him that the darkness had the upper hand, and the bulbs were desperately fighting the darkness that engulfed the place.

"One minute," said Othman.

Books were carefully arranged inside a glass newsstand, newspapers and magazines covered with pictures of women were hanging from both sides, and a bright light flashed inside the neon strip.

"I cannot sleep without reading the newspaper," said Othman. He turned on the light inside the car and handed him the paper.

"Yes. No problem," replied the prisoner, as he glanced at the headlines and quickly scanned the articles. There was a lot of disturbing news, the paper showed two big pictures of the dead and wounded. He became even tenser.

Othman stopped again and told him that he would back in few moments. The prisoner saw a butcher with a large cleaver striking the body of a sheep that dangled from a metal hook. Othman returned carrying a bag.

"Oysters on the rock for Ghada's breakfast," Othman said, then added, "When you marry, you will understand. There are a lot of demands: the wife's magazine, her breakfast, the child's milk, and on and on, my friend."

Othman concluded his statement with a laugh, which the prisoner nervously obliged with a laugh of his own, amused by the noises of the laughs that he found himself forced to produce since he left prison. The vehicle drove on.

If it were morning, everything would have been better. In the morning, there was plenty of time for thinking and arranging things, instead of being led like this, without free will—waiting when Othman waited and laughing when Othman laughed. How confused he was facing the outside world! Meanwhile, Othman was saying, "Work first, then marriage. . . . All problems will be solved . . . But you have to start soon."

"Yes. Of course," said the prisoner while looking through the newspaper and reading irrelevant little details.

"Can you believe it? One month and he already looks just like me," said Othman referring to Muqbel, his first child.

"Great, wonderful," said the prisoner.

Othman continued, "You will not understand the joy of fatherhood until you become a father yourself. I am speaking from experience."

"Of course," the prisoner confirmed. He thought: Othman's experience was definitely vast.

At that point, the door opened onto a field of light. She stood there, and he heard her say, "Welcome," and watched as she stretched out a bare arm exposed to her shoulder, covered with a shiny black dress. The dress was pitch-black, and her lips were red.

He shook her hand and said, "Thank you."

Othman raised his hand in a theatrical gesture as he introduced them to each other. Meanwhile, the prisoner was confused about what to do with his silly bag, wishing that he had left it in the prison. He walked toward the guest room, his ears still ringing with the sounds of their mixed voices. She approached. When he looked at her face again, he became consumed with its glow, and he nervously tried to find something to say.

There were paintings on the walls, light blue seats, tables of different sizes, and a mound of red apples on a glass tray. His eyes wandered, scanning the guest room. He placed his bag in the corner next to him and sat down.

"Feel as if you were in your own home," said Othman.

"At home and more," added Ghada.

The prisoner repeated, "Thank you, thank you."

She walked to where he could see her. Her back was glowing; and through her small glowing teeth, she said, "We all eventually come out of our jails."

Othman rolled up his sleeves, offered him a cigarette, and said, "Yes, of course."

The prisoner added, "And forget."

Othman said, "We quickly forget. Sometimes, when work exhausts me, I fondly remember the prison, a quiet place, and I say to myself, 'By God, those were the good days.'"

"Nice! Perhaps I will, too." The prisoner shook his head, pondering.

"The important thing is that we quickly forget," said Othman, blowing smoke out of his narrow nostrils and repeating the statement multiple times.

"And what is the thing that you should not forget?" Ghada said, laughing.

Othman clasped his hands and said, "Oysters on the rock, those, I never forget."

Ghada picked the bag and carried it to the kitchen. The prisoner listened to the tapping of her feet and imagined her black dress. He then stared at the mound of apples and quickly moved his eyes away, worried that they might see him looking.

He thought: Are all these special arrangements for me—the light brown wood shining, and the apples piled on the tray? Or is this what happens in this house every evening? What a prisoner with little experience I am!

"Tired?" Her question teased him.

He straightened his posture and answered, "No, not at all."

He stared at her small bright teeth and the dark pupils of her eyes, and realized that he was definitely exhausted. He felt the urge to think about a name for the color of her skin but obeyed an instinct that he should stop. He could not keep his eyes from following her, strolling along her arm, and exploring the rest of her body. He continued to do so while listening to the sound of Othman breathing in the washroom and the water pouring down the sink. When she moved, he saw the round tip of her shoulder, light and bright, and then noticed the small bundle of soft short hair with mysterious shadows under her arm. He raised his head; his eyes met the two dark black pupils, and he moved restlessly in his seat. Her lips were closed, but it seemed as if they were hiding a secret smile.

Othman came in, drying his face with a white towel. "How about washing your face?" Othman asked.

"I would love to."

"Man! Do you think you are still in prison? You should have asked. Remember, we said you are at home. Now, come, and stop being so polite."

He watched Othman, noticed that he was limping, and wondered if that was how he always walked. Many thoughts rushed through his head in no specific order. He was confused and wanted to be alone in the bathroom to sort out his thoughts and feelings. But there he was again, instead of trying to understand the reason for his tension and anger, his eyes wandered aimlessly around the place. He was impressed that the bathroom was much cleaner than he had expected.

2.

The table was light brown, and the food was placed on the glass panel that covered the wood. The centerpiece of the meal was a rooster sitting in a tray, broiled to perfection, his neck raised a little and bent down. At the end of it, the head was still hanging, buried in the soft noodles. The noodles surrounded the rooster's body on all sides. There were white salads, green salads, red salads, and other small plates, the contents of which he did not recognize.

"Ghada prepared her favorite meal for you," Othman said. "And for the prisoner is the chair at the head of the table."

"A great meal!" He took the white napkin from her hand, and stared at the miserable rooster burying his head in the noodles, a rooster with no dignity left.

Othman said, "Offer him some food, Ghada, and get him out of his daydreams."

She grabbed a thigh, tilting the rooster and sinking his beak farther into the noodles. She put it on his plate and added a mixture of salads.

"And you as usual, will be eating the breast," said Othman, as he served himself the other thigh.

She took off a piece of the breast and said, "The breast tastes better, even though most people like the thighs."

When she moved her arms, the prisoner noticed the top of her shoulder and the edges of the soft darkness under her arm, and he swallowed his food with difficulty.

Othman said, "You have to eat like a prisoner who was just released from prison. The amount you eat will determine how much you will please Ghada."

"The food is delicious!"

The metal utensils ringing on the glass, the sound of sucking on the bones, the colors of the food, the black glow of her dress and eyes, the white shimmering of her skin, even the soft noodles were all passing painfully down his throat.

Othman said, "No. I'm not happy with how much you ate. What is wrong with you, man?"

"I ate as much I could," said the prisoner.

Ghada said, "No. By God, are you upset?"

Othman said, "We all come out of prison confused. Despite what they call the darkness of prison, a man finds himself taken care of there.

He has a place. He has food. I understand you, my friend. Of course, I understand!"

The prisoner listened and tried to understand.

Othman continued, "But don't worry too much, the prisoner soon forgets and starts his new life. The beginning is very hard. I remember when I first started at the insurance company. I was a traveling salesman, going to homes and offices, talking to people for hours, trying to snag a customer so that I could make a sale and get a commission! I would talk and talk and talk. Most of the time, I got nothing but disappointment. I would sometimes think that prison is a better place. Foolish thoughts, you know!" Then Othman noticed the prisoner staring at him and said, "Why did you stop? You can listen and eat at the same time."

Ghada said, "Talking about insurance kills the appetite."

"Not at all," said the prisoner. "But I'm done. Thank you."

"As you like," said Othman, picking his teeth.

Ghada asked, "Would you like to eat the apples here or in the living room?"

"I don't feel like eating an apple now. Can we do that later?"

"Of course. So, then we'll drink the coffee there. Please go ahead and wash your hands."

In the living room Othman continued, "I will take care of finding you a job at our company, and that will save you the hassle of looking. Even the position of a traveling salesman is not that easy to find these days."

It had been a while since Othman left prison. He knew many things. The prisoner realized that he was just starting to forget and continued to listen.

"The door-to-door salesman job is hard, because people are stupid and do not understand the vital role of insurance. They all have children, and if you talk to any one of them about the future of these children, he would shake his head and say to you. 'Even animals come into the world with what God has allotted for them.' Yes, but God wants his animals to work to ensure the future of their children."

Othman was blowing smoke, consumed with an enthusiasm that surprised the prisoner and even scared him a little. From the kitchen came the sound of the pots clicking and tapping the edge of the garbage can. The head of the rooster must have been tossed there.

"But a true salesman does not give up. He tries again and again. His success depends to some degree on his ability to mesmerize his customers. So often, I would spend my time talking to an idiot, then leave empty-handed. But I would come back and try again in a different way, connect to his heart, until at last he drops the magic phrase: 'OK, write the policy.' He might regret it immediately after saying that, but it would be too late. The policy would be prepared quickly; and the first installment would be paid; and when the customer pays, the commission is due. Most stop after a few payments and lose what they put in, but this shouldn't be any of your concern."

Ghada arrived carrying the tray of hot steaming coffee. She said to Othman, "Have mercy on him, you are boring him with your insurance talk."

"Of course, what else do women do other than put down their men's work? Tell her, by God, where she would have money to eat and drink, if it wasn't for the insurance company?"

"I understand, but eight hours of insurance is enough!"

"My dear, are you jealous of the insurance agency, even though it is placed at your service?"

Ghada let out a laugh that the prisoner did not like. The conversation bothered him, and he went on drinking his coffee with little or no pleasure. Then he heard a voice like a cat's meow coming from inside.

"Ha, ha! Muqbel woke up. Bring him for our friend to see," Othman said, excited.

Ghada came back carrying a bundle with Muqbel inside it and bent down, presenting him to the prisoner who was surprised by how he looked. He immediately recalled Othman's conversation about the child.

His face was slim and long, his tongue dangled out of his mouth, and his eyes were two narrow holes.

"A gift from God; how wonderful!" the prisoner said.

It was not at all what he thought. His hypocritical words seemed distant and as strange as the strangeness of the events of the night itself.

"His father's face, 100 percent?" said Othman.

"Correct," replied the prisoner.

He closed his eyes, exhausted, hoping that darkness would fill the place and that he would fall asleep.

3.

The prisoner went to sleep and was haunted by nightmares.

Things started playfully. He and Othman were on an empty street. Othman teased him with his silly moves and silent laughs, then took off his shirt, unbuttoned the prisoner's shirt, swapped the shirts in a comical manner, and ran away. The prisoner laughed but could not hear himself. He then realized that he was apprehensive. He tried to run after Othman; and he became more fearful. He felt as if he were a stranger there and was afraid to lose sight of Othman. He watched the fog cover the place and increased his speed. He saw Othman move away and disappear beyond the curve of the road. Small rocks struck him, and he noticed two groups of children throwing stones at each other.

His nightmare went on. It started to rain. Othman's shirt was too big for him; he had not buttoned it up. The children were not able to see him, and he could not tell them to stop. So he ran with his head down, and his fear that he had lost Othman continued to escalate. The stones hit his wet head, and he touched the wounds with the palm of his hand. He noticed that his blood had mixed with the rain and was running down his face. He turned around, looking at a few of the houses around, but found no trace of Othman. He realized that he was totally alone, and he stood there, confused. A middle-aged woman approached him; he asked her to show him the way to downtown.

"Are you a stranger?" the woman asked.

"Yes."

She took him into her house, saying that he needed to dry his clothes. He sat in a modest room and tried to speak but was unable to make any sound. He just smacked his lips in a desperate attempt to make himself heard. His large tongue blocked any sounds from coming out. He waved his hands and pointed to his mouth, but the woman disappeared without doing anything about him or his plight.

· · ·

The prisoner opened his eyes and realized that he was sleeping in the guest room at Othman's house and that he was just dreaming. One minute passed, and then he fell asleep.

· · ·

In a large room with dim lights, he sat at the edge of a high couch, with his feet dangling, a beautiful woman to his right and a short man to his left. He wished to talk to the woman, but he did not know her. A tall man wearing long black trousers and a white jacket entered the room.

He said, bowing in a theatrical manner, "What would you like to eat?"

The prisoner looked to his right and discovered that the woman there was just a huge plastic doll. He saw her stiff figure, but as soon as she noticed his gaze, she moved her eyes, pretending to be a real woman. As he turned to look left, he saw the tall man still bowing. He was made of plastic, too. But he also moved as soon as the prisoner's eyes met his, and he stood tall like a real man. The prisoner was frightened and looked in all directions. His fear of their pretending accelerated, but he could not escape.

· · ·

Now, the prisoner opened his eyes for a moment, confirmed that he was dreaming, and promised himself that he would not fall asleep again. He was very scared. But he did fall asleep, and again, he fell back into the world of dreams.

· · ·

He found himself in a long white hospital. The doctor came in; he was a well-dressed giant with graying hair. The strange thing was that his head was shining, as if a very glossy substance had been rubbed on it.

The doctor ordered him to stretch out and rest. He repeated that he should rest, nothing else.

The prisoner said, "I am willing to tell my life story."

The doctor said, "No, no. It is early. You need to rest."

The prisoner tried to rest. Meanwhile, the doctor sat by his feet and started to tickle the bottoms of his feet. Again, the prisoner said, "I'm ready to tell my life story."

The doctor smiled and continued to tickle the bottoms of his feet. Then suddenly, he rose up and violently pushed the table the prisoner was laying on and said, "Anesthetize him."

The prisoner continued to gesture with his hands that he wanted to tell his life story.

"Open your mouth," the doctor screamed, while giving him a shot of anesthetic.

The prisoner's eyes were bulging, and his teeth were big. The prisoner opened his mouth, and the doctor pushed the needle into his lower jaw.

"Bad teeth," said the young nurse.

They started to crush his lower teeth; the nurse pulled out the remaining roots with her fingers.

The giant doctor appeared, so the prisoner raised his finger to explain that he was ready to tell his life story. He kept his finger raised but could not speak. The giant doctor passed by and paid him no attention. He watched as the doctor grabbed a white cloth bag to put over his head.

He continued to scream without a voice, "I am not crazy! This is a mistake! I am not crazy!"

As soon as he opened his eyes, he got up. He supported himself, garnering all his strength to prevent himself from falling.

4.

A few hours must have passed until the morning broke. He did not sleep again until the first light of the morning approached. That was when he felt safe enough to go back to sleep.

Her footsteps were tapping the floor of the living room, and her voice hummed a song that he did not recognize. It was obvious that the sun had reached its zenith outside. He moved his body, let out a cough, and felt a murky calmness engulf him. Two and a half footsteps preceded her appearance at the opening of the door.

"Good morning."

"Good morning," he answered, straightening his posture.

Smiling, she asked him, "Do you like milk with your coffee?"

"Oh, yes. Please."

She left the room with a smile and a wink, her head was bending down toward her chest, and her body was blossoming under the white pajama top that sparkled with impressions of small flowers.

"A black lily closed at night, and a carnation opened in the morning," he thought. He was pleased to have found these patterns and realized that he was still alert, despite all of the nightmares.

She approached him, carrying a tall glass with steam rising from it, and bent over him. He was able to see more of the stretch of her neck that led to the tip of her cleavage. Delicious waves moved through his fragile body.

"How was your night?"

"Ah, fine, fine."

She sat close to his stretched out legs at the edge of the wooden bed, graceful, free, like a wild mare.

He took a few sips from his cup and stared at it, waiting for her to say something. She said, "You needed sleep."

"Othman advised me to leave you alone until you woke up on your own."

"Thank you. Where is Othman?"

She laughed and said, "Where? At the insurance company, of course."

She spoke effortlessly, tapped her feet on the wood, and smiled.

"You like sleep, just like Muqbel." She fixed her gaze at him as if she were hammering a nail into his soul.

He liked the comment, and to keep the conversation flowing, he said, "Muqbel is weak, why?"

"It is possible that the milk does not suit him, I tried all brands in the market, but to no avail. This is a problem."

"But why?" he asked enthusiastically, "Why the milk in the market? Your milk has more nutrition."

"His father wants me to save my milk." Her look hammered more nails into his soul.

He asked angrily, "But why?"

"I don't know. Ask him that question." She stood up while dropping a sharp smile at him. She bent over to pick up the cup and said, "Your bath is ready."

She left. The sound of her steps striking the floor left him wondering what was going on in her beautiful head.

5·

The fire raged inside the furnace. He tried to balance the water coming out from the two water faucets. He did not want hot water or cold water. He lay down trying to relax in the bathtub, which was painted a color he found hard to define. It was not exactly pink or plum. It was something in between.

He did not want to feel the sting of the hot water; so he opened the cold-water faucet. He did not want lukewarm water, however. It seemed hard for him to get the exact temperature that he was looking for.

At the same time, he became occupied with a piece of silk lingerie hanging above him on a golden hook. He thought about it time and again.

It was like a flag waving over him; nonetheless, it was nothing but a black piece of clothing.

The prisoner was not aware that the perfect temperature that he was trying to reach was 98.6°F.

The tub was perfectly smooth. The two faucets were within his reach, and he was lying down. The small thought of trying to rest consumed him. He tried hard to reach that state but failed.

It was not exactly that it was unattainable. It was just his exhausted, frail body—in the tub, under the pinch of the high heat, the bite of cold water, and the dullness of the lukewarm water and that cruelty, the black flag—tormented him. Actually, it was the cruelty of it all combined.

How could he have known that the temperature he was seeking was 98.6°F? Even if he knew, what good would that do him? He would not be able to create that exact temperature in that tub no matter how many times he tried. The prisoner was disoriented.

He nearly forgot everything of the world of the prison he had just left behind. He could hardly believe that he was once there. But a dull gloominess pierced him, like the quick penetration of a dagger. He was not aware of its presence.

Again, that dullness and the water that could never reach the right temperature he sought contributed to the way he felt.

This in its entirety did not please him. He was unable to be at peace with himself, so he interrupted his uncomfortable relaxation and dried his body off, feeling sorry for himself, sorry for his weak body.

He smiled sadly while wearing Othman's borrowed clothes, loose clothes that folded around his body and made him feel lonely inside.

When he came out, she met him with a greeting.

He said, "Thank you."

He turned his face to avoid looking at her. He was tired. He didn't want her to give him any more tormenting smiles. He didn't want her to hammer more nails into his soul. He was a tired man, nothing else. He was surrounded by an overwhelming feeling of self-pity for the man inside the loose clothes borrowed from Othman.

She said to him, "Breakfast is ready."

He glanced at the white glass dishes. There were fried eggs, fried goat testes, fresh yogurt, white cheese, a white glass pitcher with steaming tea, and empty cups.

The stack of apples from yesterday was still there. Which yesterday? Othman and his wife both ate apples yesterday, while he made excuses and did not. This all seemed a distant memory.

He sat at the table, eating slowly, and felt the bites pass down his throat with difficulty.

"What is wrong with you?" She asked, with the glimpse of that penetrating smile still lingering in her eyes.

He wondered why things had to be that way. Her smile seemed tense, with harshness that he did not want to feel, just like the black flag hanging on the golden hook. Why? Why?

The prisoner was consumed by the thought of sleep. Not necessarily sleep, but the need to relax and rest.

"Nothing, nothing at all," the prisoner replied.

Really, there was nothing; all that he wanted was to rest.

"No, you are anxious."

When he heard that, he felt as if he were kicked. Why? Why was she so sure of herself? Yes. He was tired, but he did not want to hurt anyone. What a big difference between her piercing smile and the man in him who would not react to anything because he was miserable and wanted to rest. He gratefully thought about the fried eggs, the fried goat testes, all the food on the table, and the preparation time that went into it. Still, he had no interest in engaging with anyone.

She said to him, "You didn't eat anything. Are you being shy?"

He said, "No. Honestly, I ate as much as I could."

"You don't like my food?"

He said, "I swear, I ate as much as I could."

Did he eat as much as he could? Or, was it that her food and all the preparation that went with it did not please him?

He did not know. He should have been eating with a great appetite. Definitely fried eggs and fried goat testes were not a poor man's meal.

In her white pajama sprinkled with flowers, she smiled and asked again. At that point, he wished he knew what was wrong with him. Why did he have no appetite?

No, he actually was not well. Why? He did not know exactly what was bothering him. He wished he knew. Instead, he walked to the sink miserably and washed his hands, even though they were not dirty; and he walked around in his baggy clothes, without understanding what was exactly happening to him.

He took one of Othman's cigarettes.

"May I?" he asked with a lump in his throat.

She gave a premeditated, calm answer. "Please."

He lit the cigarette and lay down on the long couch, smoking.

Dull, the blurriness overwhelmed him. He lay there silently and smoked. She was free, taking the dishes to the kitchen. Why the kitchen? Why the plates? Why? Why? Why?

Why should the rooster's head remain attached to his body while he was being roasted? Why?

Yes, he was slaughtered and roasted. No one should have been angry but . . . only . . . yes . . . that beak was beautiful and actually gentle. Once he used to crow at dawn, or it might not have been exactly at dawn. He would peck and ride the neck of his hens with joy. He had a nice beak. Yes, not beautiful, that would have been vain. Nothing was intentional. No one was against anyone. It just happened. It was a kind rooster, but there was a need for him to be eaten. If you would have discussed the matter with him and said, "It was necessary that a beautiful rooster be slaughtered," he probably would have accepted that. It was clear that roosters had to be killed sometimes.

That was fine; it was fine. No one should get upset about that—but to go and piss on the grave of a dead being. Why? Why?

The prisoner was tired. He was smoking Othman's cigarette, and all that he wanted to do was rest. She finished cleaning the table. She was agile and kind; her white pajamas sparkled with flowers. Flowers were inherently kind. Certainly, if there were a common language between flowers, roosters, and people, they all would have understood each other. The flowers would have said, "I am happy to be picked. I will adorn the entrance of the house." The rooster would have said, "It is not sad that we are butchered. People love us, and they invite each other to feasts made from our bodies." The people would have said, "We did not want to harm anyone, but the flowers are beautiful, and the roosters are delicious." Perhaps everyone would have laughed with tremendous joy.

The prisoner was smoking and thinking. When she finished cleaning the table, she returned. She moved with grace, effortlessly, and sat next to him on the couch. He moved, giving her more space to sit.

She said, "House chores are harder than men think."

To hell with what men think; he did not give much weight to their controlling thoughts and actions. He gave up part of his comfortable space for her, and he was happy doing that.

She asked, "May I have a cigarette?"

He opened the box, took one out, and lit it for her. She was so beautiful.

She looked like a flower when she was not being snobbish. She said, "You didn't have much breakfast. That was not eating."

He said, "Not at all. I am grateful."

She laughed, emboldened again. He became sad. What turned him off? All his thoughts might have been wrong; he was a confused man; it was hard for him to trust his thoughts.

She said to him, "You seem sad."

She simply stretched out her hand and held his. That worried him. Yes, he was truly worried, but he did not know why.

He said, "I don't know! There is something wrong with me."

She went on asking, "Why are you sad?"

She was still holding his hand, and there was warmth, and then more warmth; and that was what he wanted. Not the scorching heat, not the biting cold, not a lukewarm feeling. She looked at him with no more arrogance in her eyes, nothing but warmth.

He said, "Nothing. I am not sad."

She said, "Poor you."

That was warmth, and now he was no longer anxious; he was almost relaxed. He raised her hand a little, trying to kiss it, not meaning any harm. All what he wanted was to be close and warm. He felt a little resistance while trying to raise her hand, but he continued, hoping to be warm again. When it had almost reached his lips, she pulled her hand in a quick and unexpected jerk and moved away from him to the other side of the couch.

That surprised the prisoner. He felt the gloominess tightening its grip on him. He didn't know the source of the blurriness that engulfed him, he felt as if the room around him was frozen in time, and he didn't know why. He did not understand what had happened. His mood was not hot or cold or lukewarm, but a dull and extended blurriness, nothing else.

But why? Why? Dullness and nothing else? He wondered. She was still there, on the other side of the couch.

Why?

He pulled his body slowly toward her and continued to wait. At last, he reached her and held her hand. Blurriness and dullness stretched to the end of the world.

He held her hand again, but he was far away, so he crawled with his small body until his mouth reached her mouth, and he said, "Please."

She was not smiling, but she fixed her gaze on him. He was not fully aware of what was happening and heard his voice saying to her, "Please."

Tired, he reached for her mouth. He knew that her eyes were lowered, looking at him. He had no time to feel shame, so he repeated, "Please." He threw his head back as he tried to close his eyes.

"No," he heard her dry voice say, and he realized that she was pulling away.

His attempt to lie down had failed. He did nothing but watch himself retreat, while she pulled herself to the other side of the couch.

Nothing went through the prisoner's head. His body immediately withdrew as he attempted to comprehend the whole ordeal. This pushed him to the verge of laughing. It was the first thing that went through his head, to laugh. He didn't know why he should laugh, so he didn't. Instead, he pulled his small body back to where it had all started. He shrunk in his seat and tried to lie down as he had earlier. He knew that she could see him from where she sat and could watch his uncomfortable position and possibly mock him and laugh at his attempt to return to his normal rhythm. There were some things that he lost control of and didn't pay too much attention to. He realized that his loud panting could be heard and that his heart was pumping harder than it should. But he knew that all of that would soon end. He was confident that his organs, moving in chaos, would go back to working as normal soon. She looked at him intensely; her glance seemed urgent! He did not understand.

Rather than the synapses of his brain operating efficiently to figure out what was going on, the sight of the rooster with his head dangling in the noodles flashed back in his head. The absurd thought that there was a stifled cry in the beak of the slaughtered roasted rooster persisted.

What a head I carry on my shoulders! The prisoner thought. I want to understand.

The truth was that the prisoner wanted help of a different kind. He wanted to understand. He wanted the disorder in his heavy breathing and his racing heart to gradually get back to normal.

Yes, what is happening? The prisoner thought. I want to understand.

Now, he forced his brain to work. He tried to get to the bottom of things by tracing the sequence of events. Leaving prison at the wrong time, yes, that was where the problem started. He then dismissed that because he had no control over it. He was released at the end of the day. He had no choice in deciding the hour; no prisoner ever decides on the hour of his release. No. That was not exactly the problem. Then, there was Othman receiving him.

Was Othman happy to see him? Was he as interested in him as he appeared to be? So, why wasn't he happy? Wasn't happiness a pulse that moved from one heart to another?

Then, there was the open door, the black dress moving, the tingling. What did he think? Was all of that special celebration for him? Who was he to deserve it? Yes, then the roasted rooster. Was that for him, too? After that, there was the mound of apples and the statement, "as if you were in your own home." He had no home. Yes, he had no home. So how did that make him really feel? Then? Yes? What? He remembered then, there was the bag. Where was the bag?

"Please where is my bag?"

"Do you need something from it?"

He was delighted by the charm of her smile. She was still in control of her voice. In contrast, his question sounded more like a cough. Then, he added, "I would like to make sure it is safe."

"Is there something in it that you are concerned about?"

"Then you opened it?"

"There is nothing important in it."

He let out a loud, deep sigh and felt ashamed. She must have opened the bag, and that was why she knew that there was nothing important in it. Regardless, it was his bag, and he was not at all comfortable with anyone opening it, especially her. It was his private property. This was too much for him. No prisoner would have wanted his bag opened.

"Would you be happy if some opened your bag?" His interrogating voice had a new tone: an accusatory tone.

He repeated, "Would you like that? Say, would you like it if someone opened your bag and went through it?" She didn't answer.

He continued, "Regardless if there was something in it or there wasn't. Let us assume that it was totally empty. Would you like to have your bag opened without your permission?"

He could see her clearly. A cloud seemed to be covering his eyes; tears were building up in them.

"O my God! Why? Why?"

His two clinched hands hit the couch next to him and produced nothing but the bouncing of the foam. He dropped his head and heard himself weeping but still asking the question. What was it that made him continue to ask while sobbing?

"Why? Why?" He felt her weight over him and two eyes watching his chest.

Her voice penetrated him, asking, "Are you angry at me? I am sorry. I didn't mean to."

He wished that the weight would go away and that her hands would not try to lift him. Her voice was sharp, like a knife cutting through his loud cry. Even his cry was now violated.

No matter what, he would have liked to continue to weep for at least a few more minutes. Where did all of that go? He was being lifted like a sack of flour.

She pulled him, rested his head on her chest, raised his chin with her left hand, looked down at him with a gaze, and said in a soft voice, "Don't be angry with me."

She tapped his face with two fingers. It did not make any noise, unlike the wood of the bed, which made a noise when she tapped it with her feet. "You cry over a bag with nothing important in it?"

She ran her hand across the front of his neck.

"No one likes his bag opened in his absence."

His childlike voice surprised him. He didn't want to be lifted off her chest, but his sensibility wanted a more comfortable place for his head. He wished that everything could have been different, but he wanted this too.

"OK. What about you? Didn't you try to kiss Othman's wife in his absence? You see? We all do the same things." He felt the light pressure of her hand while she asked, "Should I make you a cup of coffee?"

The pressure from her hand suggested that she wanted him to move away from her chest. He responded immediately, and he was consumed with shame at once.

"A cup of coffee would be great. Wonderful!" He sprang up, let out a broken laugh, and waved his arms in the air.

"If I knew that a cup of coffee would have pleased you so much, I would have made you ten cups."

"Would please me? O my God, nothing would please me as much as a cup of coffee, one cup, not ten. Very little satisfies me."

She went to the kitchen thinking that something strange must have happened to this man. But what? A desire to understand stirred within her. She heard him close the bathroom door. She tried to retrace in her mind his tired steps to the bathroom. Then, she pictured him there, with his peculiar smile, and recalled all that fuss over a cup of coffee. How strange men were!

He did not need to use the bathroom. He wanted to be alone to think. He felt an urgent need to think, and he was more comfortable and capable of mental process there than in the living room. Yes. He was just sitting there thinking.

"Didn't you try to kiss Othman's wife in his absence? You see?" He reexamined the question, recalling her tone and the way she looked at him, recalling glimpses of the events that took place, and realizing that he now was as far as he could be from the prison. A lifetime had passed since he left—lying in the bathtub, the silk piece left on the golden hook, his desire of water not cold not hot, and her moving where he could see her. He recalled his earlier thought, "A black lily closed at night, and a carnation opened in the morning," and he shook his head, smiling. Finally, something made him smile.

"Didn't you try to kiss Othman's wife in his absence. You see?" He saw Othman's wife, but he did not think about her being that. He thought only about the black lily and the carnation. What a silly thought.

He chuckled. She was not Ghada or a lily or any such thing but Othman's wife. This was the missing part of the puzzle. The missing piece was that he did not see anything related to Othman. Othman and his world were totally absent from his mind. He did not want to kiss Othman's wife, but he wanted to kiss her. How could he do that if she was labeled "the virtuous wife"?

This was what they called a wife under these circumstances. How miserable he was. Now he had to think of his world without lilies, without her. He was a man, fresh out of prison. Othman was an employee at the insurance company, married to this woman, and they had a child together. What a terrible looking Muqbel! Why did his father keep his milk from him? Damn such a father! A man with that beautiful suit, capable of roasting a whole rooster with its head still attached, fed on Muqbel's milk! He was the same Othman that greeted him at the gate of the prison. Othman, the righteous one, was willing to hire him at the insurance company. That same Othman had a child who looked like a lizard; and he drank the child's milk! He thought, "How does he drink it; directly, like a kid drinking from a goat or from a cup?"

He was aware that she was Othman's wife. He thought of Othman's offer, if he would accept it. He would gradually move from being a door-to-door salesman into Othman's position; then, he would get his own wife and have a child. He did not want lizards. No. No more lizards. He never liked lizards. The only problem he had was that she was a "virtuous wife."

Now this problem had to be resolved. He wished that he had realized what was really going on when he first got himself into this. Then he would have saved himself from this intense feeling of dullness, confusion, and chaos. Things were of utmost clarity now.

She heard him washing when she entered the living room, carrying the coffee tray. It was strange that he turned the water faucet on all the way.

She placed the tray on the table and waited until he came out. He turned to the table, picked up a red apple, and took a bite. This was also a strange thing to do.

He asked, "Would you like an apple?" She was surprised.

"No. Thank you. I don't like apples," she answered, worried about the way he was acting.

"Even though they are red and shiny, they leave an aftertaste." He swallowed the first bite and followed it with another.

"But you are eating it."

"It is okay to have one or two bites but not more. Its taste is not encouraging."

What was happening to the man? He was talking about her apples in that rude way. The strange thing was that the changes in him happened suddenly. She felt like slapping him and kicking him out of the house.

"Did you ever eat tastier apples?" She asked him nervously.

He threw the apple away and said, "No."

"Then how do you know that it has a bitter taste if you haven't tasted anything sweeter?"

The prisoner walked to her confidently and said, "I can appreciate the taste of good apples. However, I took two bites. I didn't reject it."

He repeated that and moved another step toward her, then stopped. She looked at him like a small leopard. Her scent wafted, and he felt totally defenseless. Sudden shivers consumed him, and his heart started beating faster. The problem was not just his heartbeat: his teeth chattered, and his breathing bellowed like a pump. He tried to control the chaos in his nerves as she bent over him, splashed with flowers, powerful, smiling. Now! he said to himself.

It happened in an instant; all in his mind.

He lifted her shirt and freed the top part of her body with a swift move. She threw her legs in the air and said, "No. No."

His internal voice returned. She trembled between his hands and then pushed him away. He threw her on the couch and held her tight, while she said, "No."

He wished that he could stop moving in that hideous way. An internal wave of heat swept through him. He bent with closed eyes, wiped his face with her nakedness, and kissed her.

She said, "Othman might come."

He said nothing, held her tight, and kissed her again, not knowing where his kisses fell exactly. His hands relaxed a little. Her movement started to subside until it totally stopped. Silence spread. His face went over the length of her nakedness, with his eyes still closed. He raised his head and saw her looking at him calmly.

Then she said in a different tone, "Othman might come."

He said, stuttering, "Don't be afraid."

He hoped that he wouldn't have to speak again. He squirmed a bit, freeing himself from half of Othman's clothes. He held her calm body and buried his head in her neck.

He never had held anything as tight as this, his fingers clinging to her shoulder. His soul had never trembled like this before. His soul seemed to pour out of his limbs. He had the urge to call out with a loud voice, to call her name. Meanwhile, his hip bones were cracking with sharp pain. He wished that his hips would break and dissolve. Then he calmed down. His body was oozing with sweat. He kissed the front of her neck calmly, ran his face on it, heard her rhythmic breathing, and yearned to look at her.

He raised a tired glance and saw her looking over him. Her eyes were open, watching him. No smile, no anger, just two eyes watching. A feeling of agony and shame swept over him. And, while his breath was reeling in miserable chaos and his fingers clinging to her, she continued to watch him. Everything he did was nothing more than a comical performance—in reality, a failed performance. Woe to his tiny insulted figure, he the small clown that no one wanted.

His hunger, his desire to call her name, his oozing sweat, and everything else was nothing but a small and ridiculous lie. But, this face had a scent, a softness that could not lie. She could be a flower, or even prettier. So why? Why?

Her voice brought him back, "You are tired?"

"Yes, very tired. I did not sleep last night."

"Was the bed uncomfortable?"

"No, not the bed. The bed was comfortable. The nightmares were awful and exhausting."

"Nightmares?"

"Plastic men and women."

She laughed.

"Devious men, all made of plastic, but they appeared as if they were men of flesh and blood."

"Why?"

"I don't know."

"When I see them, they pretend to be alive; and when I am not looking, they go back to being plastic." He laughed nervously.

"Do you have to be sad?"

"Yes, I believe I do have to be sad."

"What is making you sad?"

"Your scent."

She laughed.

"Do you like expensive perfume?"

"No. To hell with expensive perfumes." Then he added, "They broke my teeth and wanted to suffocate me."

"Who wanted to suffocate you?"

"The figures in my nightmares."

"Don't be sad."

"I won't be sad, if you really don't want me to be sad."

"I want that."

"You're pretty. Don't be made of plastic. What's good in that?"

"There's no good in that at all."

"So?"

"Sometimes, sometimes, it is very pleasurable—I mean to be plastic."

"And the others? I mean, they don't realize that?"

"They don't know. What about you? Don't you like Othman?"

"I don't think I like him. I can't. I am sorry."

"Don't be sorry."

"I want to like him, believe me. But I can't."

"Don't be sorry, I don't like to see you in his clothes."

"I will take them off. I will take them off right away."

"Poor thing, your body is very skinny when you are naked."

"You have to love it."

"I love it. I do love it."

He continued to unbutton her buttons. He held her like a treasure between his arms and went over her softness with his hand—black wet petals, a flower in its cup, a bouquet of black flowers, a naked woman.

She said, "I am happy."

He moved the palm of his hand over her nakedness and realized that her hips were soft but strong.

He said to her, "You are delicious, like a ripe fruit."

He kissed her all over her body, and she helped him in his journey, touching his nakedness with the palm of her hand.

"You are even prettier when you close your eyes. How generous you are."

She said, "It feels as if I am on a swing."

She met him with a warm and wide celebration. Her body moved like waves, and a soft music played.

They both closed their eyes and allowed the soft warm waters to complete the ritual, a free swing, soaring up high. The blueness of the sea was wild, and the sea had a white foam. It rushed toward them, shielded them, and washed over them with a tremendous joy. His cries woke the dawn of the primitive earth. A man was united with a woman, and a woman was united with a man, perfect like two halves of a grain of wheat.